Praise for *The Desert of Love*

"This translation into English of one of Mauriac's outstanding early novels comes with the impact of a book strictly contemporary with our own times. . . . One sees again that M. Mauriac, who surely ranks among the very greatest of novelists in this century, is the aphoristic novelist par excellence. This Pascal of novelists, as Graham Greene calls him, unites again and again the specific incidents of his story with superb reflections and generalizations about the human heart."—*Catholic World*

Other François Mauriac novels available from Carroll & Graf:

Viper's Tangle
The Woman of the Pharisees

The Desert of Love

FRANÇOIS
MAURIAC

The Desert of Love

TRANSLATED BY GERARD HOPKINS

Carroll & Graf Publishers, Inc.
New York

First published 1951 by Pellegrini & Cudahy
Farrar, Straus and Cudahy edition published 1958.

First Carroll & Graf edition 1989

Reprinted by arrangement with Farrar, Straus & Giroux, Inc.

Carroll & Graf Publishers, Inc.
260 Fifth Avenue
New York, NY 10001

ISBN: 0-88184-485-3

Manufactured in the United States of America

The Desert of Love

1

FOR YEARS Raymond Courrèges had been cherishing the hope that one day he might run across Maria Cross, the woman on whom he had so ardently longed to be revenged. Often in the street he would follow some chance passer-by, thinking to have found her. But in the course of time the edge of his resentment had become blunted, so that when, at length, they did come face to face, he felt, at first, none of that joy shot with fury which such a meeting should have stirred in him.

It was only ten o'clock when he entered the bar in the rue Duphot. The colored jazz band was playing softly for the delectation of a solitary waiter. Over the tiny floor which, when midnight came, would be crammed with dancing couples, a ventilating fan was making a noise like a gigantic bluebottle. To the doorman, who said, with a look of surprise, "Don't often see you here as early as this, sir," he replied with no more than a wave of the hand, which conveyed a wish that something should be done to stop this intrusive bumbling. The man did his best to explain, confidentially, but without success, that the new system "absorbed the smoke without causing a draft." Courrèges gave him such a look that he beat a hasty retreat to the cloakroom. Up in the ceiling the ventilator droned to silence, as though a bee had suddenly alighted.

The young man sat down at one of the tables, thus breaking the immaculate vista of white cloths. A glance in a mirror showed him that he was not looking his best. What's the matter with me? he wondered. God! How he hated a wasted evening—and all because of that swine Eddy H——. He had had to dig the fellow out and almost drag him to a restaurant. During dinner Eddy had scarcely listened to what he was saying, and had excused his inattention on the ground of a sick headache. He had sat perched on the very edge of his chair, impatience in every line of his body, obviously preoccupied with the thought of some happiness to come. No sooner had he finished his coffee than he had taken eagerly to his heels—eyes shining, ears flushed, and nostrils flaring. Raymond had spent the day in delighted anticipation of their dinner and of the evening that was to follow it. But, no doubt, Eddy had in prospect pleasures more stimulating than any offered by a mere exchange of confidences.

Courrèges was amazed to find that he felt not only disappointed and humiliated, but also sad. The discovery that the companionship of a friend to whom he attached no particular importance could show as thus precious to him came as a shock. It was something entirely new in his life. Up to the age of thirty, being quite incapable of the selflessness demanded by true friendship, and devoting much of his attention to women, he had disregarded everything that was not an object to be possessed, and, like a greedy child, would have said, had he put the feeling into words, "I like only what I can eat." At that period of his life he made use of his cronies either as witnesses of his conquests or as recipients of his confidences. He looked on a friend as, first and foremost, a pair of ears. He liked, too, the feeling that he could dominate them and control their actions. Influencing others had become a passion with him. He flattered himself that he had reduced the demoralizing of his companions to a fine art.

Raymond Courrèges could have built up a big career for himself, as his grandfather the surgeon had done; his uncle, the Jesuit, and his father, the doctor, if only he had been capable of harnessing his appetites to work, if only his natural tastes had not led him to concentrate all his energies on the achievement of immediate satisfaction. But by now he was reaching the age at which only those who address themselves to the soul can set their dominance on a firm foundation. The best that Courrèges could do for his disciples was to assure them a quick yield in terms of pleasure. But the younger men of his acquaintance preferred to share their adventures with others of their own age, and his circle was growing thin. In the preserves of love there is no shortage of game, but we soon find that the little group of those in whose company we set out grows smaller year by year. Those who had survived the dark violence of the war had either dwindled into husbands or had their natures distorted by the pursuit of a calling. He noted their graying hair, their protuberant bellies, their bald pates, and hated them because they were the same age as himself. He accused them of having murdered their youth, of having betrayed it even before it had fled from them.

It was a matter of pride with him to be taken for a "post-war product"; and this evening, in the still empty bar, where the only sound was the muted thrumming of a mandolin (the flame of the melody rising, falling, flickering), he studied with fierce attention the image thrown back at him from the mirrors, the image of a face with a thatch of vigorous hair on which his thirty-five years had not yet set their mark. It came to him, as he pondered, that age would lay hands upon his life long before it touched his body. If it bolstered up his self-esteem to hear women say among themselves—"Who's that tall young man?" he knew that the keener-eyed twenty-year-olds no longer thought of him as forming one in their ephemeral group. Maybe Eddy had had something better to do than talk about himself to an accompaniment of wailing saxophones; on the other hand, he might be doing just that at this very moment in some other bar, laying bare his heart to some youth born in 1904, who would constantly interrupt the flow of his talk with "me, too," and "that's just what I feel. . . ."

A number of young men began to drift in. They had assumed expressions of self-conscious arrogance preparatory to crossing the floor, and were now, at sight of the empty room, visibly embarrassed. They gathered in a little cluster round the bar. But Courrèges had made it a rule never to let himself suffer because of the behavior of others—whether mistresses or friends. True, therefore, to this principle, he set himself to stress the lack of proportion existing between the insignificance of Eddy H—— and the feeling of uneasy restlessness which was the legacy left behind after that young man's defection. . . . He was pleased to find that this weed of sentiment, when he tried to pull it out, came away without any difficulty. He wound himself up to the pitch of thinking how little it would mean to him, next day, to show his friend the door. He even contemplated without concern the possibility that he might never set eyes on him again. It was almost with a sense of gaiety that he thought, I'll wash my hands of him once and for all. He sighed with relief, only to find that a sense of unease remained which had nothing whatever to do with Eddy. . . . Ah, yes, of course, that letter! He could feel it in the pocket of his evening jacket. No point in reading it again. Dr. Courrèges, in communicating with his son, made use of a telegraphic brevity of expression which was easily remembered:

Staying at Grand Hotel duration Medical Congress. Available mornings before nine, evenings after eleven.

Your father,
PAUL COURRÈGES

"Not if I know it!" he murmured, unaware that his face had taken on an expression of defiance. He held it against this father of his that it was less easy to despise him than the other members of the family. On reaching the age of thirty, Raymond had demanded a lump sum down comparable to what his sister had received on her marriage. But in vain. Faced by the parental refusal, he had burned his bridges and taken himself off. But it was Madame Courrèges who held the purse strings, and he knew perfectly well that his father would have acted generously by him had he been in a legal position to do so, and that money meant nothing to the old man. "Not if I know it!" he said to himself once more, but could not, for all that, help catching the note of appeal which sounded in the dry little message. He was far less blind than was Madame Courrèges, who felt only irritation at her husband's undemonstrative nature and brusque manner. "He may be a good man, and he may have a heart of gold," she was fond of saying, "but what good is that to me if I never get a glimpse of it? Just think what he would be like if he was *bad!*"

Just because it was so difficult to hate his father, Raymond found these claims upon his affection hard to endure. He wasn't going to answer the letter. All the same. . . . Later, when he thought back to the circumstances of this evening, he remembered the bitterness of his mood when he entered the deserted little bar, but forgot what had caused it—the defection of a friend called Eddy, and his father's presence in Paris. He believed that his sour ill temper had been born of a presentiment, and that a connection existed between the state of his emotions, on that occasion, and the event which was fast approaching. He always later maintained that neither Eddy nor the doctor was, in himself, capable of getting him worked up like that, but that, from the very moment he had settled down with a cocktail, some inner voice, some clamor of the flesh, had warned him of the imminent appearance of the woman who, at that same moment, in a taxi which had already reached the corner of the rue Duphot, was rummaging in her little bag, and saying to her companion:

"What a bore! I've forgotten my lipstick!"

To which the man replied, "There'll probably be one in the ladies' room."

"What a mad idea! one might catch . . ."

"Well then, get Gladys to lend you hers."

She came into the bar. A cloche hat completely obliterated the top part of her face, leaving visible only her chin, that feature on which time sets the sign-manual of age. Forty years had, here and there, touched this lower segment of her countenance, drawing the skin tight and sketching a hint of sagging flesh. Her body beneath its furs must, one felt, be shrunken. As blind as a bull brought suddenly from its dark pen into the glare of the arena, she stopped short on the threshold of the glittering room. When her companion, who had been delayed by a dispute over the fare, rejoined her, Courrèges, though not at once recognizing him, said to himself: "I've seen that fellow somewhere—bet he comes from Bordeaux"; and then, suddenly, as he looked at the face of the man of fifty, swollen, as it were, by the sense of its own identity, a name formed itself on his lips: Victor Larousselle. . . . With beating heart he resumed his examination of the woman who, quickly realizing that no one else was wearing a hat, had taken off hers, and was shaking out her freshly cropped hair in front of a mirror. He saw, first of all, a pair of eyes that were large and calm: next, a wide forehead, its limits sharply marked by the seven youthful points of her dark hair. All that remained of the legacy of youth seemed concentrated in the upper part of her face. Raymond recognized her in spite of the short hair, the middle-aged "spread," and nature's slow work of destruction, which, beginning at the neck, was busy invading the areas of mouth and cheeks. He recognized her as he would have a road familiar to him in childhood, even though the oaks once shading it had been cut down. He calculated the lapse of time. The sum took him a bare two seconds. She's forty-four, he thought; I was eighteen and she was twenty-seven. Like all those who confound the ideas of happiness and youth, he had a consciousness of the passage of time which was ever active, strive though he might to keep it muffled. His eye was forever measuring the sundering gulf of the dead years. He at once inserted in life's chronology every human being who had played a part in his existence. No sooner did he see a face than he could supply a date.

Will she recognize me? he wondered. But would she have so sharply turned away if she had not already done so? She went up to her companion and seemed to be begging him not to stay, for he replied very loudly, and in the tone of a man who craves an admiring audience, "What nonsense! it's not a bit gloomy. In a quarter of an hour it'll be as tight packed as an egg with meat!" He pushed out a table not far from the one at which Raymond was leaning on his elbow, and sat down heavily. The blood had rushed to his face, sure sign of hardening arteries. But apart from that its expression was one of unruffled satisfaction. The woman was still standing motionless. "What are you waiting for?" he asked. Gone, suddenly, from the eyes, from the coarse and purplish lips, was all look of pleasure. In what he thought was a low voice, he said: "It's enough for me to like being here for you to start sulking—of course!" She must have told him to be careful, have warned him that he could be overheard, for his next words were almost shouted: "So I don't know how to behave, don't I? What does it matter if they *do* hear?"

Seated not far from Raymond, the woman seemed to have recovered her composure. In order to see her the young man would have had to lean forward. It was for her now to avoid his eyes. He realized her renewed sense of security, and was made suddenly aware, with a quick feeling of terror, that the opportunity which, for the last seventeen years, he had so eagerly desired might slip through his fingers. He thought that he was still, after all that time, determined to humiliate the woman who had so deeply humiliated him, to show her what manner of man he was—the sort that doesn't let a bitch get the better of him without hitting back. For years he had found pleasure in thinking what would happen when fate at last should bring them face to face, how he would skillfully contrive matters so as to ride roughshod over, and reduce to tears, the woman in whose presence he had once cut so ridiculous a figure. . . . Doubtless, if tonight he had recognized not this woman, but some other trivial familiar of his eighteenth year—the boon companion of that distant time, the miserable usher whom he had loathed—he would, at sight of them, have found in himself no trace either of the affection or of the hatred, now outgrown, which the callow schoolboy had then felt. But, faced by this woman, did he not feel now just as he had felt on that Thursday evening of 19—, when he had walked in the fading light along a dusty suburban road smelling of lilies, and stopped before a gate whose bell would never again ring to the pressure of his finger?

Maria! Maria Cross! Of the shy and grubby youth he had been then she had made a new man, the man he was to be forever after. How little she had changed! The same questioning eyes, the same radiant forehead. Courrèges reminded himself that his favorite school friend of 19— would, by this time, be heavy, prematurely bald, and bearded. But the faces of a certain type of woman remain steeped in childhood until well on into maturity, and it is that quality of childhood, perhaps, that produces in us a fixation of love kept inviolate from the weapons of time. There she was, as she had always been, after seventeen years of passions about which he knew nothing, like one of those black Virgins whose smile the flaming fanaticisms of Reform and Revolution have been powerless to change. She was still being "kept" by this same man of substance who was noisily venting his ill-humor and impatience because the people for whom he was waiting had not yet turned up.

"I expect it's Gladys as usual who's making them late. . . . I'm always on the dot myself . . . can't stand unpunctuality in others. I suppose I'm odd in that way. I just can't bear the thought of keeping other people waiting—some sort of an instinct, I suppose—no use fighting against it. But good manners are a thing of the past. . . ."

Maria Cross laid a hand on his shoulder, and must have said again: "Everyone can hear what you're saying," because he growled out that he wasn't saying anything he minded people hearing, and that it really was a bit too much *her* teaching *him* how to behave.

Her mere presence had the effect of delivering Courrèges bound hand and foot to the vanished past. Though he had always had a keen sense of days long gone, he had a hatred of reviving the memory of their details, and feared nothing so much as the shuffle of ghosts. But he could do nothing this evening to disperse the crowding procession of faces brought by Maria's presence to the surface of his consciousness. He could hear again, in memory, the clock striking six, and the banging of desk lids in Upper School. Not enough rain had fallen to lay the dust: the light in the trolley was too bad for him to finish reading *Aphrodite*—in the trolley filled with workpeople to whose faces the exhaustion of another day had imparted a look of gentleness.

2

HE WAS a grubby brat. Much of his time at school he spent being turned out of the classroom, wandering about the passages or leaning against old walls. When he left it in the evening, and before he got to his suburban home, there was a long interval of time, spent, most of it, in the trolley, which stood in his mind for freedom, for deliverance. At last he could feel himself alone, surrounded by indifferent faces and incurious eyes. This especially was so in winter, because then the darkness, shredded only at intervals by scattered street lamps and the glare of occasional bars, shut him away from the world, isolated him in a universe that reeked of damp working-clothes. Dead cigarettes dangled from sagging lips; faces seamed with coal dust lay tilted back in sleep; newspapers slipped from hands gone numb; a hatless woman held up her novelette to catch the light of the lamps, her lips moving as though in prayer. But the end of the journey came at last, and, just after they had passed the church at Talence, he had to get out.

The trolley—a moving Bengal candle—lit up for a few brief moments the yews and naked elm branches of a private park. Then the boy heard the noise of the trolley wheels diminish as he stood in the puddle-pocked road. His nose was filled with the scent of rotting wood and leaves. He turned up the lane that ran by the Courrèges garden wall and pushed open the half-closed gate leading to the back yard. The light from the dining-room window lay across a clump of bushes where, in spring, the fuchsias were planted, because they love the shade. At this point in the return journey his face took on the sullen look it wore at school; his eyebrows drew together till they showed as a single matted line above his eyes, and the right-hand corner of his mouth began to droop. Entering the drawing room he threw a collective "Good evening" to the occupants, who sat grouped about a single niggardly lamp. His mother asked how often must he be told to wipe his feet on the scraper, and did he mean to sit down to dinner with his hands "like that"? Madame Courrèges, the elder, murmured to her daughter-in-law: "You know what Paul says: don't nag the boy unnecessarily." His very appearance seemed to start an exchange of bitter words.

He sat down where the light could not reach him.

Crouched over her embroidery, Madeleine Basque, his sister, had not so much as raised her head at his entrance. He was of less interest to her, he thought, than the dog. In her opinion, Raymond was the family's "running sore." "I don't like to think what *he'll* grow up into," she was forever saying, to which her husband, Gaston Basque, would contribute his mite by adding: "It's all because his father's so weak."

She would look up from her work, sit for a moment with her ears pricked, say suddenly, "There's Gaston," and lay aside her task. "*I* don't hear a thing," Madame Courrèges would remark. But—"Yes, it's him," the young woman would repeat, and then, though no sound had reached any ear but her own, would run out onto the terrace and disappear into the garden, guided by an infallible instinct, as though she belonged to a species of animal different from all others, where it was the male, and not the female, who exhaled the odor that would draw his partner to him through the darkness. In a moment or two the Courrèges' would hear a man's voice followed by Madeleine's gratified and submissive laughter. They knew that the couple would not come back through the drawing room, but would use a side door and go straight upstairs to the bedroom floor, from which they would not descend until the gong had been sounded twice.

The company round the dining-room table, beneath the hanging lamp, consisted of the elder Madame Courrèges, her daughter-in-law, Lucie Courrèges, the young couple, and their four little girls, all with their father's reddish hair, all dressed alike, all with the same complexion and the same patches of freckles. They sat huddled together like tame birds on a perch. "No one's to say a word to them," ordered Lieutenant Basque. "If anyone addresses them, it's they who will be punished. Now don't say I didn't warn you."

The doctor's chair remained empty for some considerable time, even when he happened to be at home. He would come in halfway through the meal, carrying a bundle of learned journals. His wife said, Hadn't he heard the gong? and complained that with everything in the house at sixes and sevens, it was quite impossible to keep any servant for long. Shaking his head, as though to chase away a fly, he proceeded to bury himself in one of his journals. This was not affectation on his part, but merely a way of saving time devised by a man who was in a constant condition of overwork, never free from worries, and fully aware that every minute was precious. At the other end of the table, the Basques sat isolated and aloof, supremely indifferent to everything that did not directly concern either them or their little ones. Gaston would be explaining how he was pulling strings to avoid being moved from Bordeaux, how the Colonel had written to the Ministry . . . his attentive wife all the while keeping a watchful eye on the children and maintaining an uninterrupted flow of educative comment: "Don't you know how to use a knife?" "Don't sprawl." "Keep your hands on the table—hands, I said, not elbows." "Now mind what I say, you won't get any more bread." "You've had quite enough to drink already."

The Basques formed an island of secrecy and suspicion. "They never tell me anything"—all Madame Courrèges' grievances against her daughter could be summed up in that phrase—"they never tell me anything." She suspected that Madeleine was pregnant, kept a careful eye on her figure, and drew her own conclusions when the girl complained of not feeling well. The servants, she maintained, always knew everything before she did. She believed that Gaston had taken out an insurance policy on his life, but for how much? She had no idea what money they had come into on old Basque's death.

In the drawing room, after dinner, when she grumblingly inquired whether Raymond hadn't any homework to do, any essay to write, he made no answer. He would take hold of one of the little girls, look as though he were about to crush her in his great hands, toss her up over his head so that she could touch the ceiling, and swing the lithe little body round and round, while Madeleine Basque, like a ruffled and uneasy hen—though disarmed by the child's excitement, would exclaim: "*Do* be careful; I'm sure you'll do her some injury"; and then, turning to the company in general, would remark: "He's so *rough*," at which Grandmamma Courrèges, laying down her knitting and pushing up her spectacles, while her whole face crinkled into a smile, would at once embark on a brisk defense of Raymond: "Why, he *adores* children," she would say. "You can't deny that children are all he cares about . . ." for it was one of the old lady's convictions that he wouldn't be so devoted to them if he hadn't a heart of gold. "You've only got to see him with his nieces to realize that there's nothing really to worry about."

But did he really care so very much about children? The truth was he made use of anything that came his way, provided it was warm and living, as a weapon against those whom he called the "corpses." Depositing the young body on the sofa, he would, on these occasions, make for the door, rush from the house, and stride along the leaf-encumbered paths.

Between the branches a lighter patch of sky guided his steps. Doctor Courrèges' lamp glowed from behind a window on the first floor. Should he go to bed without looking in on his father to say good night? The three-quarters of an hour of hostile silence each morning were all that he could stand. Every day, early, the brougham set out, carrying father and son. Raymond got out at the Barrière de Saint-Genès, from which he walked, by way of the boulevards, to school, while the doctor continued on to the hospital. For three-quarters of an hour they sat side by side in a smell of ancient leather, between streaming windows. The doctor, who a few moments later would be speaking eloquently, authoritatively, to his helpers and his students, had been vainly seeking for months some word that would provoke a response from this being of his own flesh and blood. How was he ever to succeed in blazing a path to this heart which was always bristling with defenses? Each time he congratulated himself on finding a joint in the young man's armor, and began speaking to Raymond in phrases planned long in advance, his words seemed suddenly like the words of a stranger: his very voice, dry and mocking, had, he felt, turned traitor—no matter how hard he tried to make it sound natural. This powerlessness to give expression to his feelings was his habitual martyrdom.

It was only through his actions that Dr. Courrèges' kindness of heart was widely recognized, for they alone bore witness to the good that lay so deeply embedded in him that it was like a man entombed. He could never hear a word of gratitude without a growl and a shrug. Bumping along through rainy dawns beside his son, he was forever addressing silent questions to the withdrawn and sullen face there at his elbow. In spite of himself he could not help interpreting the signs that showed upon that face as those of some dark angel—the deceptive sweetness, for instance, that he caught in eyes that were more deeply shadowed than they should have been.

The poor boy regards me as his enemy, thought the father, and the fault is mine, not his. But he was reckoning without the sure instinct for those who love him which is forever active in the adolescent. Raymond heard the unvoiced appeal, and never confused his father with the others. But he deliberately turned a deaf ear to what never found release in words. Nor could he, on his side, have thought of anything to say to the victim of shyness at his side, for the effect of his presence was to numb the older man with timidity, and so turn him to ice. Nevertheless, the doctor could not refrain, now and again, from remonstrating with him, though he always did so as gently as possible, and in terms of a friendship between equals.

"I've had another letter about you from the headmaster. Poor Abbé Farge, you'll really send him out of his mind! It seems to be proved without a shadow of doubt that it was you who passed round that treatise on obstetrics—I suppose you sneaked it off my shelves. I must confess that his air of outraged virtue seems to me somewhat excessive. After all, you're old enough now to know about the facts of life, and it's a good deal better that you should get them from solid, scientific books. That's the line I took in my reply. . . . But I gather, too, that a number of *La Gaudriole* was found in the newspaper rack in Upper School, and, very naturally, you are under suspicion. All the sins of Israel are laid to your charge. Better look out, my boy, or you'll find yourself expelled with the final exams still a good six months off."

"No."

"What do you mean—no?"

"Because I'm working extra hard and stand a good chance of not being flunked a second time. I know their sort! They're not going to get rid of the only fellow who's likely to pass. Besides, if they showed me the door, the Jesuits would snap me up in a jiffy! They'd far rather let me go on contaminating the others, as they put it, than run the risk of losing a good item in the school records. Think how triumphant old Farge will look on Speech Day: thirty candidates—twenty-three 'Honors' and two 'Passes.' . . . Thunderous applause. . . . What a lot of swine they are!"

"No, my boy, that's where you're wrong." The doctor stressed those words, "my boy." Now, perhaps, was his opportunity to penetrate the lad's stubborn heart. For a long time his son had obstinately refused to show the slightest sign of weakening. The glow of a trusting confidence showed through the cynical words. What should he say that might have the effect, without putting the boy on the defensive, of proving to him that there *are* men who don't resort to tricks and calculations, that sometimes the cleverest are those Machiavellis of high causes who wound us when they wish us well? . . . He felt about in his mind for the most suitable formula, and even while he pondered the problem, the suburban road had turned into a city street filled with the bright and melancholy radiance of morning and the jostle of milk carts. A few moments more and they would reach the city limits, that Croix de Saint-Genès where once the pilgrims to St. James of Compostella had knelt in momentary adoration, and where now only bus inspectors leaned against the walls. Unable to find any suitable words, he took the other's warm hand in his, said in a low voice, "My boy" . . . and then noticed that Raymond, his head pressed to the window, was asleep, or pretending to be asleep. The young man had closed his eyes, perhaps for fear that they might, for all his efforts to the contrary, betray a weakening, a desire to yield. He sat there, his face fast shut to all approaches, a bony face that looked as though carved in granite, in which the only sign of sensitiveness was the vulnerable line of the eyelids.

Very gradually the doctor withdrew his hand.

Was it before that scene in the brougham, or later, that the woman sitting over there on the settee, separated from him by no more than a single table, so that he could have spoken to her without raising his voice, had come into his life? She seemed calmer now, and was sipping her drink with no fear, it seemed, that Raymond might have recognized her. Every now and again she looked at him, only to look away almost at once. Suddenly her voice—and how well he remembered it!—rose above the babble of noise: "There's Gladys!"

The newly arrived couple came over at once and sat down between her and her companion. They all started talking at once. "We were waiting for our cloakroom tickets." "We're always the first to arrive—well, anyhow you've come, that's the main thing."

No, it must have been more than a year before the scene between father and son in the brougham that one day at dinner (it would have been in the late spring, because the lamp in the dining room had not been lit) Madame Courrèges the elder had said to her daughter-in-law: "I know whom the white hangings in the church were for, Lucie."

Raymond had thought that one of those endless conversations was about to begin, full of trivial phrases that dropped dead about the doctor's chair. As a rule, they had to do with household matters, each of the women present rushing to do battle for her own particular member of the staff, so that the encounter became a squalid Iliad in which the quarrels of the servants' quarters set the various patron Goddesses at one another's throat in the Olympus of the dining room. Often the two families would set about disputing the favors of the daily sewing woman. "I've arranged with Travaillotte to come to me next week," Madame Courrèges would say to Madeleine Basque, and then the younger woman would at once protest that the children's underwear needed mending.

"You always grab Travaillotte."

"Well, then, why don't you get old broken-nose Mary?"

"Broken-nose Mary is a much slower worker. Besides, she always insists on my paying her carfare."

But on this particular evening, the mention of the white hangings in church had given rise to a more serious discussion. Madame Courrèges the elder had more to say.

"They're for that poor little boy of Maria Cross's, the one who died of meningitis. I gather she ordered an extremely expensive funeral."

"How very tactless!"

At his wife's exclamation, the doctor, who sat reading a journal while he drank his soup, raised his eyes. She, as usual when that happened, lowered hers, angrily remarking that it was a pity, all the same, that the curé hadn't managed to instill some sense of guilt into a woman who, as everyone knew, was a kept creature, who flaunted her shame all over the place, with her horses and carriages and all the rest.

The doctor made a gesture with his hand indicative of protest.

"It's not for us to judge: she's done *us* no harm."

"What about the scandal? I suppose that doesn't count?"

From his face she could see that he was saying to himself how vulgar she was. She made an effort to moderate her tone, though a few seconds later she exclaimed as loudly as before that women like that gave her the horrors. . . . The house that for so long had been the home of her old friend, Madame Bouffard, Victor Larousselle's mother-in-law, was now occupied by a slut. . . . Every time she passed the door it cut her to the heart. . . .

The doctor, speaking very calmly, and in an almost hushed voice, interrupted the flow to point out that the only person in that house tonight was a mother sitting by her dead child. At this, Madame Courrèges, with one finger raised, announced solemnly:

"It is God's judgment!"

The children heard the scraping sound made by the doctor's chair as he pushed it sharply back from the table. He thrust his journals into his pocket, and, without another word, walked across to the door. He forced himself to move slowly, but the family, all attention now, could hear him running upstairs four steps at a time.

"Did I say anything so very extraordinary?" Madame Courrèges addressed a questioning look at her mother-in-law, at the young couple, at the children, at the servant. The only sounds in the room were the scraping of knives and forks and Madeleine's voice: "Don't nibble your bread—stop playing with that bone. . . ."

Madame Courrèges, her eyes fixed on her mother-in-law, said: "I really think he must be ill."

But the old lady, her nose buried in her plate, seemed not to have heard. It was at this point that Raymond burst out laughing.

"If you must laugh you'd better go outside! And don't come back till you can control yourself!"

Raymond threw his napkin on the floor. How peaceful it was in the garden. Yes, it must have been late spring because he remembered the bumbling noise made by the cockchafers, and that they had had strawberries for dinner. He had sat down in the middle of the paddock on the still warm stone rim of a fountain which no human eye had ever seen spouting water. He noticed his father's shadow passing and repassing the windows of the first floor. In the twilight that poured dusty and heavy over this stretch of country not far from Bordeaux, a bell was tolling at long intervals because death had come for the child of this same woman who now sat drinking so close to him that he could have stretched out his hand and touched her. Since starting on the champagne, Maria Cross had been gazing more boldly at the young man, as though she were no longer afraid that she might be recognized. To say that she had not aged was an understatement. In spite of the fact that she had cut her hair, and that she was wearing nothing that trespassed beyond the winter's fashion, her whole body had somehow kept the lines that had been in vogue about 19—. She looked young, but it was as though her youth had come to flower fifteen years ago and remained unchanged. She was young in the way that no one is young today. Her eyelids looked no wearier than they had when she had said to Raymond: "Our eyes have a fellow feeling."

Raymond remembered how, on the morning following the evening on which his father had suddenly left the table, he had sat very early in the dining room drinking his chocolate. The windows were open on the dawn mist, and he shivered a little. There was a smell of freshly ground coffee. The gravel of the drive crackled under the wheels of the ancient brougham. The doctor was late. Madame Courrèges, in a purple dressing gown, her hair plaited and twisted in the way she always wore it when she went to bed, kissed him on the forehead. He went on with his breakfast without pausing.

"Isn't your father down yet?"

She said that she had some letter to give him to mail. But he could guess the reason for her early appearance. When the members of a family live cheek by jowl, they get into the habit of never giving away their own secrets but of ever being on the alert to probe the secrets of others. The mother said of her daughter-in-law: "She never tells me anything, but there's little I don't know about her." Each person in the group claimed to know all about the others, while remaining inscrutable himself. Raymond thought he knew why his mother was there: "She wants to make it up." After a scene like that of the previous evening, she would dog her husband's footsteps, seeking to be taken back into favor. The poor woman was always discovering too late that she had the fatal gift of habitually saying what would most get on the doctor's nerves. As in certain forms of nightmare, the more she tried to approach him, the farther away she seemed to get. She could do nothing, say nothing, that was not hateful to him. Tangled in her clumsy efforts at tenderness, she was, as it were, always groping her way forward with outstretched hands. But whenever she touched him it was to bruise.

As soon as she heard the sound of his bedroom door closing, she poured out a cup of steaming coffee. A smile lit up her face, which was marked by the traces of a sleepless night and worn by the slow dripping of laborious and identical days. But the smile vanished as soon as the doctor appeared. She was already on her guard, trying to read the expression in his eyes.

"Why, you've got your top hat and overcoat on!"

"That is quite obvious."

"Are you going to a wedding?" . . . "A funeral, then?"

"Yes."

"Who has died?"

"Someone you don't know, Lucie."

"Tell me who it is."

"The little Cross boy."

"Maria Cross's son? Do you know her? You never told me you did. You never tell me anything. Considering that we were talking at dinner of that hussy . . ."

The doctor was drinking his coffee, standing. He answered in his quietest tones, which was always a sign with him that he was exasperated almost beyond bearing, though well under control.

"Haven't you learned, even after twenty-five years, that I prefer to discuss my patients as little as possible?"

No, she hadn't, and insisted that it always amazed her to find out, quite by chance, in the course of a social call, that this or that friend of hers had been attended by Dr. Courrèges.

"It's so awkward for me when people look surprised. 'What,' they say, 'do you really mean to tell me that you didn't *know?*' and then I have to admit that you don't trust me, that you never tell me anything. Were you treating the child? What did he die of? I can't see why you won't tell me. I never repeat things. Besides, with people like that, what can it matter? . . ."

For any sign the doctor gave, he might not have heard or seen her. He put on his overcoat, calling to Raymond: "Get a move on; seven o'clock struck ages ago."

Madame Courrèges pattered along behind them.

"What have I said now? You suddenly put all your prickles out. . . ."

The door slammed. A clump of shrubs hid the brougham from view. The sun began to shred the mist. Madame Courrèges, talking disjointedly to herself, turned back toward the house.

Seated in the carriage, the schoolboy looked at his father with eager curiosity, anxious for confidences. Now, if ever, father and son might have drawn closer together. But the doctor's thoughts were far from the boy with whom, so often, he had longed to come to grips. Here was the young prey ready to his hand, and he did not realize it. He sat there, muttering into his beard, as though he had been alone: "I ought to have called in a surgeon. One can always try trepanning as a last resort." He pushed back his top hat with its nap all brushed the wrong way, lowered one of the windows, and thrust out his hirsute countenance above the traffic-encumbered road. At the city limits he said absent-mindedly: "See you this evening," but he did not gaze after Raymond's retreating form.

3

IN THE course of the following summer Raymond Courrèges had his seventeenth birthday. He remembered it as a season of torrid heat and shortage of water. Never since then had the city of stone lain prostrate under so intolerable a glare, cluttered though his memory was with many summers spent in Bordeaux, a city protected by hills from the north winds, and close invested by pines and sand which concentrated and accumulated the heat—Bordeaux, so poor in trees, except for its Public Gardens, where, to the eyes of children parched with thirst, it seemed as though the last vestiges of green in all the world were being burned to cinders behind the tall and solemn railings.

But perhaps, in retrospect, he was confusing the sun's heat of that particular summer with the inner flame that was burning him up, him and sixty others of his age, who had their being within the limits of a yard separated from other yards by the back walls of a row of latrines. It needed the constant presence of two monitors to control this herd of boys who were dying into life, of men on the verge of being born. Responsive to the thrust of painful growth, the forest of young lives put forth, in a few short months, spindly and ailing shoots. The world and its ways had the effect of pruning the rank growth of these young scions of good families, but in Raymond Courrèges the action of the rising sap was fierce and uninhibited. He was an object of fear and horror to his teachers, who kept him with his scarred face (because his tender skin could not endure the razor) as far as possible from associating with his fellows. The good boys of the school looked on him as a "dirty beast" who carried photographs of women in his notecase and read *Aphrodite* (disguised as a prayer book) in chapel. He had "lost his faith." This phrase caused as much terror in the school as would, in an asylum, the rumor that one of the most dangerous lunatics had broken out of his strait jacket and was wandering stark naked through the grounds. It was matter of general knowledge that on those rare Sundays when he was not being "kept in," Raymond Courrèges hid his school uniform and his cap, with the monogram of the Virgin, in a bed of nettles, put on an overcoat bought ready-made at Thierry and Sigrand, clapped on his head an absurd bowler which made him look like a plain-clothes policeman, and hung about the more disreputable booths at the fair. He had been seen on the merry-go-round hugging a slut of indeterminate age.

When, in the pompous setting of Commencement day, an attendant multitude of parents sat stupefied by the heat in the shade of leaves already shriveled by the sun, and heard the headmaster announce that Courrèges had "passed with distinction," he alone knew what an effort he had made, in spite of the apparent lawlessness of his days, not to be expelled. A single fixed idea had filled his mind to the exclusion even of the sense of persecution, so that the hours of detention, spent standing against the rough-cast wall of the playground, had actually seemed short—the idea of departure, of flight, in the first glow of a summer morning, along the highroad to Spain which ran past the Courrèges' garden, a road that looked as though it were weighed down by the bulk of its great flagstones, a relic of the Emperor, of his guns and of his convoys. He savored in anticipation the heady delight of every step that should put a little more distance between him, the school, and his depressing family. It was an understood thing that on the day he passed his examination his father and his grandmother would each give him a hundred francs. Since he had already saved up eight hundred, he would thus be owner of the thousand which, so he thought, would enable him to travel through the world, miles and miles from his own "people." That was why he had spent the hours of detention working, untroubled by the sight of others at play. Sometimes he would shut his book and chew the cud of daydreams. In imagination he could hear the scrape of cicadas in the pine trees along the roads which soon he would be traveling, could see the cool shade of the inn before which, tired out with traveling, he would sit in some unidentified village. The rising moon would wake the cocks, and off he would start again in the freshness of the dawn, with the taste of bread in his mouth. And sometimes he would sleep beneath a mill, a single cornstook blotting out the stars: and the damp fingers of the early day would rouse him. . . .

But, though teachers and parents had agreed in thinking him capable of anything, he had not, after all, taken to flight. His enemies, though they did not know it, had been too strong for him. Defeat comes to the young because they let themselves be so easily convinced of their own wretched inadequacy. At seventeen the most undisciplined of boys is only too ready to accept the image of himself imposed by others. Raymond Courrèges was blessed with good looks, but thought himself a monster of ugliness and squalor. He was blind to the fine contours of his face, and convinced that he could rouse in others only feelings of disgust. He was filled with a horror of his own person, and felt assured that he could never pay back in kind the emotion of hostility which he caused in those about him. That was why, stronger even than the longing to escape, he felt the desire to hide, to veil his face, to be compelled no more to wipe away the hatred of future enemies yet unknown. This youthful debauchee, whose hand the pupils of the Church School were afraid to touch, was no less ignorant than they of women, and could not conceive that he might be capable of giving pleasure if only to a slattern in the gutter. He was ashamed of his body. It never occurred either to his parents or to his teachers that all his glorying in wildness and dirt was but the miserable bravado of the young which he assumed because he wanted to make them believe that he reveled in his own uncomeliness. His attitude was no more than the threadbare pride of adolescence, a sort of despairing humility.

The holidays that followed his examination, far from opening a way of escape, were a period of secret cowardice. Paralyzed by timidity, he thought he could read contempt in the eyes of the servant girl who did his room, and quailed before the brooding look which, at times, his father turned on him. Since the Basques were spending August at Arcachon, he had not even the consolation of the children with whose young bodies, supple as growing plants, he loved to play so roughly.

As soon as the young family had gone, Madame Courrèges heaved a sigh of relief.

"It's nice to have the place to ourselves for a bit," she said, in this way taking her revenge on a remark of her daughter's to the effect that "Gaston and I really need a little course of solitude."

Actually, the poor woman lived for nothing but the daily letter, and could not hear the muttering of a storm without seeing in imagination the whole Basque family being dashed to destruction in an open boat. The house was only half-full, and the empty rooms weighed heavily on her spirits. Of what comfort to her was a son who spent his time running wild about the roads, and came back sullen-tempered and dripping with sweat, to dash at his food like a ravenous animal?

"People say, 'Well, you've got your husband.' My husband! —I ask you!"

"You forget, darling, how busy Paul is."

"He doesn't have any rounds to make, mother. Most of his patients are on holiday."

"Not his poorer patients. Besides, he's got his laboratory work, the hospital, and all those articles he has to write. . . ."

The embittered wife shook her head. She knew that her husband's active temperament would never lack employment, that never, till the day of his death, would there be a moment's pause in which, for a few brief instants, she might count on his whole and undivided attention. It never occurred to her that such a thing could be possible. She did not know that in even the fullest lives love can hollow out its little nest; that the harassed statesman will stop the wheels of the world when the moment comes for his mistress to pay him a visit. This ignorance spared her much suffering. Though she was only too familiar with the kind of love that dogs the feet of someone beyond the power to touch, someone who will not so much as turn his head to take a moment's notice, the mere fact that she had always been powerless to hold his attention for no matter how brief a while made it impossible for her to imagine that for some other woman the doctor might be a totally different person. She would have hated to think that somewhere a woman might exist who was capable of charming him from that incomprehensible world in which he lived, made up of statistics and observations, of blood and pus imprisoned between glass slides; and it was many years before she discovered that there were evenings when the laboratory remained deserted, when the sick had to wait in vain for the man who, when he might have eased their pain, preferred to stand motionless in a dark and stuffy drawing room gazing down at a woman stretched upon a sofa.

In order to contrive such secret oases in his days of toil the doctor had to work with twice his normal intensity; had to hack his way through every kind of obstacle that he might win as his reward those few moments filled with concentrated watching and impassioned silence, when to look was all the satisfaction he desired. Sometimes, just when the long-expected hour had almost sounded, a message would reach him from Maria Cross saying that she was no longer free, that the man on whom she was dependent had arranged a party in some restaurant on the outskirts of the city. When that happened he would have found the thought of life intolerable had she not added a postscript to her note suggesting another day. Then, in a flash, the miracle occurred, and at once his whole existence centered about the thought of the new meeting promised by her words. Though every hour of every day was filled with duties, he included in a single sweeping act of vision, like a skillful chess player, all the possible combinations that might enable him so to arrange matters so that, when the time and date arrived, he could be there, motionless and disengaged, in the stuffy and encumbered room, gazing at the figure stretched upon its sofa. And when the moment came and went at which, had she not put him off, he might have been with her, he was filled with happiness, thinking: "It would have been over by now, but, as things are, I still have that happiness in front of me. . . ." There was something then with which he could fill the empty days that lay between. At such times the laboratory in particular took on the quality of a haven. Within its walls he lost all sense of the passing hours, even of love itself. Absorbed in research, he felt freed from time, filling with work the moments that must be lived till, suddenly, the longed-for hour would come when he could push open the gate of that small house where Maria Cross lived behind the church at Talence.

Devoured by his obsession, he gave, that summer, less and

less attention to his son. He who had been made party to so many shameful secrets often said to himself: We always think that the happenings tucked away in newspaper paragraphs don't concern us, that murders, suicides, and scandals are what come to other people, while, all the time . . . And yet, all the time, he did not know that there had been moments in the course of that devastating August when his son had been within an ace of taking an irreparable step. Raymond longed to run away, but longed, too, to hide, to become invisible. He could not pluck up courage to go into a café or a shop. He would walk up and down a dozen times before a door before he could bring himself to open it. This mania made all flight impossible, though he felt stifled in his home. There were many evenings when death seemed to him to be the simplest of all solutions. He would open the drawer in which his father kept an old-fashioned revolver, but it was not God's will that he should find the cartridges. One afternoon he walked between the drooping vines down to the pond that lay beyond the sun-baked paddock. He hoped that the weeds, the growing water plants, might knot a tangle round his feet, that he might be unable to extricate himself from the muddy liquid, that his eyes and mouth might be filled with slime, that no one might ever see him again, nor he see others watching him. Mosquitoes were skimming the surface, frogs were popping in the eddying shadows like so many stones. Caught in the weeds a dead animal showed white. What saved Raymond then was not fear but disgust.

Fortunately, he was not often alone. The Courrèges' tennis court was a focus of attraction for all the young people of the neighborhood. It was one of Madame Courrèges' grievances that the Basques should have involved her in the expense of having it made, and then, when they might have played on it, had gone away. Only strangers got the benefit of it. Young men in white, with rackets in their hands, moving inaudibly on sandaled feet, appeared in the drawing room at the hour of siesta, greeted the ladies, barely bothered to ask after Raymond, and went out again into the glare which echoed soon to their cries of "Play" and "Out," to the sound of their laughter. "They don't even trouble to shut the door," grumbled Grandmother Courrèges, who thought of nothing but keeping out the heat. Raymond might have been willing to play, but the presence of the young women frightened him —especially of the Cosserouge girls, Marie-Thérèse, Marie-Louise, and Marguerite-Marie, all three fat and fair and suffering from headache because of the weight of their hair, for they were condemned to wear upon their heads enormous structures of yellow tresses imperfectly secured with combs and always on the point of falling down. He hated them. Why must they always laugh so much? They were in a constant state of wriggling convulsions, convinced that everybody else was a "scream." They didn't, as it happened, laugh more at Raymond than at anybody else, but it was his particular curse to feel himself the center of a universal derision. But there was one reason, in particular, why he hated them. The day before the Basques went away, he had found it impossible any longer to refuse to keep a promise he had made to his brother-in-law that he would ride a monstrous great horse that the lieutenant was leaving behind in the stables. He was at the age when no sooner was he in the saddle than he was seized with giddiness. Consequently, he cut a poor figure as a horseman. One morning the Cosserouge girls had come on him suddenly in a forest ride, clinging desperately to the pommel of his saddle. A moment later and he was sprawling on the sandy ground. He could never see them after that without hearing again the giggling screams in which, at that moment, they had indulged. Each time they met him they took delight in reminding him of every circumstance of that humiliating fall. What storms does teasing, however harmless in intention, raise in a young man's heart in the springtime of life! Raymond was incapable of distinguishing one Cosserouge from another, but lumped them collectively within the orbit of his hatred, regarding them as a sort of fat, three-headed monster, always sweating and clucking beneath the motionless trees of that August afternoon of 19—.

Sometimes he took the trolley, crossed the blazing inferno of Bordeaux, and reached the docks, where human bodies, devoured by poverty and scrofula, were splashing about in the stagnant water with its iridescent scum of oil. Their owners laughed, chasing one another, and leaving on the flags the faint, damp outline of their feet.

October returned. The perilous passage had been accomplished. Raymond had passed the dangerous crisis of his life. It was written that he should be saved, and indeed he was already saved when, at the beginning of term, the new school-books (he had always loved the smell of them) brought to him a sort of concentrated vision as he stood upon the threshold of the year which was to initiate him into the study of philosophy, of all the dreams and systems that have beguiled the human mind. Yes, he was to be saved, though not by his own unaided efforts. The time was near when a woman would come into his life—that same woman who, this evening, was watching him through the smoky haze and crowding couples of the tiny bar, whose wide and tranquil brow no passage of time had had the power to change.

During the winter months through which he had lived before they met, his spirit had lain in a profound torpor. A sort of dull passivity had left him weaponless. Stripped of his old aggressiveness, he was no longer the eternal whipping boy of fate. Once the holidays had passed that had tormented him with the twin obsession of escape and death, he found himself acquiescing in the expected conduct of his days. Discipline came to his assistance by making life a good deal easier. But he savored even more intensely his daily journey home, the evening passage from one suburb to another. The College gate once left behind, he plunged into the secret darkness of the damp little lane which was sometimes filled with the smell of fog, sometimes with the hard, dry breath of frost. With the sky, too, in its many aspects, he became familiar—overcast, swept clear and corroded with stars, veiled with a covering of cloud that seemed to be lit from within by a moon he could not see. And then, in a short while, would come the city limits, with the same crowd of tired, dirty, submissive men and women waiting to lay siege to the trolley. The great glowing rectangle plunged ahead into a land, half town, half country, rumbling on between pathetic little gardens that lay submerged beneath the fathoms of the winter night.

At home he no longer felt himself to be the object of a never-ceasing curiosity. General attention was now concentrated upon the doctor.

"I'm worried about him," said Madame Courrèges to her mother-in-law. "You're lucky to be able to take things so calmly. I envy temperaments like yours."

"Paul is rather overworked. He does too much, there's no doubt about that. But he has a magnificent constitution, so I'm not really concerned."

The younger woman shrugged her shoulders, making no effort to hear what the other muttered half to herself: "He's not ill, I'm sure of that. All the same, he *is* suffering."

Madame Courrèges said, not for the first time, "Trust a doctor never to take care of himself."

During dinner she kept a watchful eye on him. How emaciated his face looked, she thought, when he raised his eyes from his plate.

"It's Friday, why cutlets?"

"You need a good body-building diet."

"What do you know about it?"

"Why won't you go and see Duluc? No doctor can ever prescribe for himself."

"My poor Lucie, why have you made up your mind that I am ill?"

"You can't see yourself. Why, the mere look of you is enough to frighten one. Everybody says the same thing. Only yesterday, someone—I forget who—said: 'What *is* the matter with your husband?' You ought to take choline. I'm sure it's your liver."

"Why my liver rather than some other organ?"

Her reply was peremptory: "My impression is that it *must be* your liver."

Lucie's impression to that effect was very definite, and nothing would induce her to give it up. Her comments buzzed round the doctor like so many flies, only far more irritating: "You've already had two cups of coffee—I must tell the cook to see that the pot isn't filled. That's your third cigarette since lunch. It's no good your denying it. There are three stubs in the ash tray."

"What proves that he knows he's ill," she said one day to her mother-in-law, "is that I caught him yesterday looking at himself in the glass. As a rule, he never bothers about his appearance, but there he was, peering at his face and running his fingers over it. It was as though he wanted to smooth out the wrinkles on his forehead and round his eyes. He even opened his mouth and examined his teeth."

Madame Courrèges the elder looked at her daughter-in-law over the top of her spectacles, as though fearful of detecting upon that puzzled countenance something more than mere anxiety, something more in the nature of suspicion. The old lady had a feeling that her son's good-night kiss had recently been less perfunctory than usual. Perhaps she knew what that momentary surrender to emotion meant. Ever since he was a young man she had got into the way of guessing the precise nature of those wounds which one person alone, the owner of the hand that deals them, can cure. But the wife, though for many years frustrated in her instinct of tenderness, had thoughts only for physical ailments. Each time the doctor sat down opposite her and raised his clasped hands to his face with its look of suffering, she said:

"You really *ought* to see Duluc: we *all* think so."

"Duluc could tell me nothing I don't already know."

"Can you listen to your own heart?"

To this question the doctor made no reply. His whole attention was concentrated upon the pain at his heart. It was as though a hand were holding and just faintly squeezing it. Ah! who better than he could count its beats, for were they not the evidence of what he had just been through with Maria Cross? How difficult it was to slip a more than usually tender word, a hinted declaration, into a conversation with a woman who showed herself always so submissive, who insisted on regarding her doctor as an almost godlike creature, and forced upon him the dignity of a spiritual fatherhood!

He went over in his mind the circumstances of his most recent visit. He had got out of the carriage on the main road, opposite the church at Talence, and had walked up the puddled lane. So swift had been the progress of the dusk that it was almost dark before he reached the gate. At the far end of an untidy path a lamp threw a ruddy glow from the ground-floor windows of a low-built house. He did not ring. No servant preceded him through the dining room. He entered the drawing room without knocking. Maria Cross was lying on a sofa and did not get up. Indeed, for a second or two she went on reading. Finally:

"So there you are, doctor; I'm quite ready for you," she said, holding out both hands, and moving her feet so as to make room for him on the end of the sofa. "Don't take that chair, it's broken. I live, you know, in a jumble of luxury and squalor. . . ."

Monsieur Larousselle had set her up in this suburban villa where the visitor was liable to trip over tears in the carpet, and only the folds of the curtains concealed the holes in the fabric. Sometimes when he went to see her she said nothing. He was prevented from starting a conversation fitted to his role of suppliant lover—a conversation which he had made up his mind *must* take place—by the presence, over the sofa, of a mirror which reflected the image of a face eaten away by a mass of beard, of two bloodshot eyes dimmed as the result of constant application to a microscope, of a forehead from which the hair had already begun to recede when he was still a house physician. Nevertheless, he was determined to try his luck. One of her small hands was trailing over the edge of the sofa, almost touching the floor. He took it, and said in a low voice: "Maria . . ." Such was her confidence in him that she did not withdraw it. "I'm not feverish, doctor; really I'm not." As always, she spoke of herself. "Dear friend," she said: "I've done something of which you'll thoroughly approve. I've told Monsieur Larousselle that I no longer need the car, that he'd better sell it and get rid of Firmin. You know how it is with him, how incapable he is of understanding any delicacy of feeling. He just laughed, and said what was the point of upsetting everything merely because of a moment's whim? But I mean it, and I never use anything but the trolley now, whatever the weather. I came back in it today from the cemetery. I thought you'd be pleased. I feel less unworthy of our poor dead darling . . . less . . . less like a kept woman."

The last two words were barely audible. The eyes which she raised to the doctor's face were brimming with tears, and seemed humbly to implore his approval. He gave it to her at once, gravely, coldly. She was forever invoking him. "You're so *big* . . . you're the noblest human being I have ever known . . . the mere fact that you exist makes me believe in the reality of goodness." How he longed to protest, to say: "I'm not the man you think me, Maria; only a poor, a very poor creature, eaten up by desire just like other men. . . ."

"You wouldn't be such a saint," she replied, when he tried to put these thoughts into words, "if you didn't despise yourself."

"No, no, Maria: not a saint at all; you don't, you can't know . . ."

She gazed at him with a fixed stare of admiration, but it never occurred to her to worry about him, as Lucie worried, to notice how ill he looked. The concentrated worship which was her tribute to him made of his love a despair. His desire was walled up within this admiration. He told himself in his misery, when he was far from her, that his love could surmount all obstacles; but as soon as she was there before him, deferential, hanging on his words, he could no longer deny the evidence of a wretchedness that was beyond all cure. Nothing in the world could change the nature of their relation. She was not his mistress but his disciple. He was not her lover but her spiritual director. To have stretched his arms toward her supine body, to have pressed it to his own, would have been as mad an act as to break the mirror hanging above her head. He knew, too, with horrible clarity, that she was waiting for him to go. The realization that she was an object of interest to the doctor was, for her, a matter of pride. Surrounded by the wreckage of her life, she prized very highly the intimacy of so eminent a man. But how he bored her! He, without having the slightest idea that his visits were a burden to her, felt increasingly that his secret was becoming more and more obvious, so obvious, indeed, that only her complete indifference could explain her inability to guess it. Had Maria felt even a vestige of affection for him, his love must have stared her in the face. Alas! how utterly insensitive a woman can be when confronted by a man whom, otherwise, she may esteem and even venerate, whose friendship fills her with pride, but who bores her! Of this truth the doctor had some faint realization only, but it was enough to crush him.

He got up, cutting her short in the middle of something she was saying.

"I must say, you *are* a bit abrupt in your manner of taking leave," she remarked; "but there are so many other sufferers waiting for you. . . . I mustn't be selfish and keep you all to myself."

Once again he crossed the empty dining room and the hall. Once again he breathed in the smell of the frost-bound garden, and in the carriage on his way home, thinking of Lucie's attentive, worried face—no doubt she was already getting anxious, and would be straining her ears for the sound of his return—said to himself: The great thing is not to *cause* suffering. It's quite enough that *I* suffer: I mustn't create suffering in others.

"You're looking much worse this evening. Why *will* you put off seeing Duluc? If you won't do it for your own sake, you might at least do it for ours. You're not the only person concerned. It affects all of us."

Madame Courrèges called the Basques to witness the truth of her pronouncement. They emerged from the low-voiced conversation which they were carrying on, and obediently backed her up.

"It's quite true, Papa, we all want to have you with us as long as possible."

At the mere sound of the hated voice the doctor felt ashamed of the strength of his dislike for his son-in-law. He's really quite a decent fellow . . . it's unforgivable on my part . . . But how was he to forget the reasons he had for hating him? For long years one thing only in his marriage had seemed to be precisely as he had always dreamed it would be—the narrow cot standing beside the vast conjugal bed, and he and his wife each evening watching the slumber of Madeleine, their first-born. Her breathing was scarcely perceptible. One innocent foot had kicked off the coverlet. A small hand, soft and marvelous, hung down between the bars. She was such a sweet-natured child that they could afford to spoil her without fear of consequences, and such advantage did she take of her father's infatuation that she would play for hours in his study without making a sound. "You say she's not very intelligent," he would say; "she's much *more* than intelligent." Later, though he hated going out with Madame Courrèges, he loved to be seen in the company of the young girl. "People think you're my wife!" It was about then that he had made up his mind that the right man for her would be Fred Robinson, the only one, he felt, of all his pupils who really understood him. He already called him "My son," and was just waiting until Madeleine should turn eighteen to conclude the marriage, when, at the end of the first winter after she had "come out," she told him she was engaged to Lieutenant Basque. The doctor's furious opposition had lasted for months. No one could see any sense in it, neither his family nor the world at large. Why should he prefer a penniless young student, who came from heaven knew where, to a well-off officer of good ancestry with a brilliant future before him?

His reasons were too personal to himself to make it possible for him to discuss them. From the first moment that he had started to raise objections he felt that in the eyes of this dearly loved daughter he had become an enemy. He told himself that his death would have been a matter to her of rejoicing, that she looked on him now merely as an old wall that must be battered down so that she could join the male who was calling to her. Because he wanted to see precisely where he stood, because he wanted to be sure to what extent this child, on whom he had lavished all his affection, hated him, he had intensified his stubbornness. Even his old mother was against him and joined forces with the young people. Plots were hatched under his own roof to enable the lovers to meet without his knowledge. When, finally, he had given in, his daughter had kissed him on the cheek. He had pushed away her hair, as he used to do, so as to touch her forehead with his lips. Everyone said: "Madeleine adores her father. She has always been his favorite." Until the day of his death, no doubt, he would hear her calling him "Darling Papa." Meanwhile he must put up with this Basque fellow. But no matter how hard he tried, he could not help betraying the fact of his antipathy. "It really is extraordinary," said Madame Courrèges. "Here he is with a son-in-law who shares his views about everything, and yet he doesn't like him!" It was just this that the doctor could not forgive, this seeing all his most cherished ideas turning to caricature in the distorting mirror of the young man's mind. The lieutenant was one of those persons whose approval flattens us out, and makes us doubt the very truths for which, previously, we would have shed our blood.

"Really, Papa, I mean it. You must take care of yourself for your children's sake. You must allow them to take sides with you against yourself."

The doctor left the room without answering. Later, when the Basques had sought the refuge of their bedroom (so sacred was it held to be that Madame Courrèges was wont to say, "I never set foot in it. Madeleine has made it perfectly plain that she doesn't want me there. There are some things that don't have to be said twice; I can take a hint"), they undressed in silence. The lieutenant, on his knees, his head buried in the bed, turned round suddenly and put a question to his wife:

"Was this house part of your parents' marriage settlement? . . . What I mean is, did they buy it after they were married?"

Madeleine thought so, but was not certain. "It would be interesting to know, because in that case, should anything happen to your poor father, we should have a legal right to one-half of it."

He said no more for a few moments, and then, after a pause, asked how old Raymond was, and seemed annoyed to learn that he was only seventeen.

"What difference does that make? Why do you ask?"

"Oh, nothing. . . ."

He may have been thinking that a minor always complicates an inheritance, because, getting to his feet, he said:

"Naturally, I hope that your poor father will be with us for a long time yet. . . ."

In the darkness of the room the huge bed yawned to receive them. They went to it, just as twice a day, at noon and at eight o'clock, they sat down to table—when they were hungry.

About this same time Raymond woke in the night. Something that had a flat taste was trickling over his face and down his throat. His hand felt for the matches. He lit one, and, by its light, saw that blood was spurting from his left nostril and staining his nightshirt and the sheets. He got up and stood, petrified with fear, in front of the mirror, staring at his long thin body all speckled with scarlet. He wiped his fingers, which were sticky with blood, on his chest, and thought how funny his smeared face looked. He began to play a game in which he was both murderer and murdered.

4

THE EVENING was just like any other evening at the end of January, when, in those latitudes, winter is already on the wane. Raymond, seated in his workmen's trolley, was jarred by the sight of the woman opposite. Far from being distressed at the thought that he formed but one anonymous unit of this human freight, he enjoyed pretending that he was an emigrant in the steerage while the ship drove ahead through the darkness. The trees were coral reefs, the people and the traffic on the road outside, denizens of the vasty deep. The journey, which while it lasted kept from him all sense of humiliation, was all too short. Every one of the bodies round him was as much neglected as his own, as badly dressed. When, as occasionally happened, his eyes met other eyes, he saw in the answering look no hint of mockery. All the same, his linen was cleaner than the unbuttoned shirt, say, of the man with as much hair on his chest as a wild animal. He felt at ease among these people. It never occurred to him that one spoken word would have been enough to conjure up the desert that separates classes as surely from one another as it does individuals. But such communion as might be possible was, no doubt, achieved by this contact, this shared immersion of a trolley car driving through the suburban night.

Rough though he was at school, here he made no effort to shake himself free of the head that was bumping up and down on his shoulder, the head of an exhausted urchin of his own age whose body sagged in sleep, as loosely articulated as a bunch of flowers too lightly bound.

But on this particular evening he noticed, opposite, a woman, a lady. She was dressed in black, and was wedged between two men in greasy overalls. There was no veil over her face. He was to wonder, later, how it was that beneath her gaze he had not, at first, been conscious of that shy awkwardness which the humblest servant girl could usually produce in him. He was troubled by no feeling of shame, no embarrassment—perhaps because in this trolley car he felt himself to be without identity, and could imagine no circumstances which might establish a relation between himself and this particular stranger. But the chief reason was that her expression was entirely devoid of anything that might have been taken for curiosity, mockery, or contempt. But, Lord, how she stared! It was as though, absorbed in that concentration, she were saying to herself: The sight of this face brings consolation for all the tedium to which one is exposed in a public vehicle. Confronted by what might well be a sullen angel, I can forget the whole miserable scene. Nothing now has any longer the power to rasp my nerves. Merely to look brings me deliverance. He is like some unknown country. The lids of his eyes are a barren stretch of sea sand. Two troubled lakes lie drowsing between their bordering lashes. The ink on his fingers, his grimy collar and cuffs, that missing button—all these things are no more than the earth that dirties a ripe fruit ready to fall from the tree, and only waiting the touch of a careful hand to gather it. . . .

He, too, feeling safe because he had nothing to fear from this stranger, not even a word, since nothing had built a bridge between them, stared back with that tranquil intensity with which we gaze upon a distant planet. . . . (What innocence still clung about her brow. Courrèges, this evening, cast a furtive look at it. The radiance which bathed it owed nothing to the glare of the tiny bar, all to that intelligence which is so rarely found in a woman's face, though, when it is, how deeply it moves us, how convincingly persuades us that Thought, Idea, Intelligence are words of the feminine gender!)

In front of the church at Talence the young woman got up, leaving with the men she was deserting only the fragrance of her presence, and even that had vanished by the time Raymond reached the end of his journey. It was scarcely cold at all on this January evening. He was not even tempted to run. Already there was a promise in the foggy air of the secret sweetness of the coming season. The earth was stripped but not asleep.

Raymond, intent on his own thoughts, noticed nothing that evening as he sat at table with his family, though his father had never looked so ill. Madame Courrèges made no reference to the fact. He mustn't be "pestered," as she said to the Basques as soon as he had gone upstairs with his mother. All the same, she had made up her mind to talk to Duluc without his knowledge. The room reeked of the lieutenant's cigar. Leaning against the mantelpiece, Gaston said: "There's no doubt about it, mother: something's the matter with him." There was a military quality of command about the jerky brevity of his speech, and when Madeleine, taking an opposite line to her mother, remarked: "It may be only some temporary upset . . ." he interrupted her.

"No, Madeleine, it's serious. Your mother is quite right."

The young woman had the temerity to argue. He raised his voice:

"I say that your mother is right, and that should be enough for you!"

Up on the first floor Madame Courrèges the elder knocked gently at her son's door. She found him seated with a number of books open before him. She asked no questions, but sat knitting, saying nothing. If her silence, her reticence, became more than he could bear, if he felt the sudden need to speak, she was ready to listen. But a sure instinct kept her from forcing his confidence. For a moment he was tempted to choke back no longer the cry which was stifling him. But to speak now would mean going so terribly far back in thought, would mean telling over one by one the beads of his misery up to the moment of tonight's discomfiture. . . . How could he explain the disproportion between his suffering and its cause? What had happened would seem so trivial. It was merely that when he had called on Maria Cross at the time they had arranged, the servant told him that she had not come in. The news had inflicted the first stab of pain. He had agreed to wait in the empty drawing room where a clock was ticking—though less quickly than his heart. A lamp shone on the pretentious beams of the ceiling. On a low table beside the sofa he noticed an ash tray filled with cigarette ends. She smokes too much . . . she's poisoning herself, he thought. What a lot of books there were, but in none were the last pages cut. His eye took in the torn folds of the great curtains of faded silk. To himself he repeated: "Luxury and squalor, squalor and luxury" . . . looked at the clock, then at his watch, and decided that he would wait only another fifteen minutes. How quickly, then, did time begin to fly. That it might not seem too short, he refused to let his thoughts dwell on his laboratory, on his interrupted experiment. He got up, went over to the sofa, knelt down, and, after first glancing nervously toward the door, buried his face in the cushions. When he got up his left knee made its usual cracking sound. He planted himself in front of the mirror, touched with his finger the swollen artery at his temple, and thought to himself that if anyone had come in and seen him, he would have been thought mad. With the characteristic aridity of the intellectual worker who reduces everything to the terms of a formula, he said, "All men are mad when they are alone. Yes, self-control is active only when it is backed by the control imposed upon us by the presence of others." Alas! that one little piece of reasoning had sufficed to exhaust the fifteen minutes' grace he had allowed himself. . .

How could he explain to his mother sitting there, eager for confidences, the misery of that moment, the degree of renunciation it had demanded, the fact that it had had the effect of tearing him up by the roots from the melancholy satisfaction of his daily conversation with Maria Cross? What matters is not the willingness to confide even when we have a sympathetic listener, even when that listener is a mother. Which of us is skilled enough to compress a whole inner world into a few words? How is it possible to detach from the moving flow of consciousness one particular sensation rather than another? One can tell nothing unless one tells all. How could he expect this old lady to understand the music that sounded so deep down in her son's heart, with its lacerating discords? He was of another race than hers, being of another sex. They were separated more surely than people living on two different planets. . . . There, in his mother's presence, the doctor recalled his misery but did not put it into words. He remembered how, tired of waiting, he had just picked up his hat, when he heard the sound of steps in the hall. It was as though his whole life hung suspended. The door opened, but instead of the woman he expected he saw Victor Larousselle.

"You know, doctor, you're spoiling Maria."

Not a hint of suspicion in the voice. The doctor smiled at the sight of the impeccable figure with its full-blooded face and light-colored suit, bursting with self-satisfaction and contentment.

"What a windfall for you doctors these neurasthenics are, these *malades imaginaires*. No, no, I'm only joking. Everyone knows what a selfless fellow you are. . . . Still, it's a bit of damn good luck for Maria that she should have happened on so rare a bird of the species as you. Do you know why she isn't back? Just because she's given up the car—that's her latest fancy. Between ourselves, I really think she's a bit touched—but that's only an added charm in a pretty woman, eh? What do you think, doctor? I must say I'm very glad to see you. Look here, stay to dinner: Maria will be delighted: she adores you. You won't? Well, at least wait until she gets back. You're the only person I can talk to about her."

"You're the only person I can talk to about her." . . . That sudden outburst of tormented words from this fat, resplendent man! This passion of his, said the doctor to himself, as he drove home, is the scandal of the place. All the same, it is the one noble sentiment of which the fool is capable. At fifty he has suddenly discovered that he is vulnerable; that he can suffer because of a woman whose body he has almost certainly conquered. But that is not enough for him. Somewhere, outside his world of business and horses, there will henceforward be a finer principle of suffering. . . . The romantic conception of passion is not, perhaps, as silly as we think it. Maria Cross! Maria! What misery not to have seen her! But even worse than that is the knowledge that she didn't even think of sending me word. How small a place I must occupy in her life! She can break an appointment without so much as a thought . . . I cram infinity into a few short minutes that for her mean nothing. . . .

The sound of spoken words roused him from his reverie. His mother could bear the silence no longer. She, too, had been following the drift of her secret preoccupations, and was no longer dwelling upon her son's load of mysterious sorrow. She was back once more with what so constantly obsessed her—her relation with her daughter-in-law.

"I let her trample on me; I never say anything but 'Have your own way, my dear, do just as you want.' Nobody could say I provoke her, but she's forever throwing her money in my teeth. Money! as though you didn't make enough! I know, of course, that when you married you had nothing but your future to offer her, and that she was a Voulassier of Elbeuf—though their mills in those days weren't anything like what they have become since. All the same, she could have made a better match, I realize that. . . . 'When one's got something, one always wants more'—as she said to me one day about Madeleine. But let's not complain. If it wasn't for the servants, everything would be all right."

"There are few worse things in life, my poor, dear mother, than having servants of different masters all living together in the same kitchen."

He touched her forehead with his lips, left the door ajar so that she could see her way, and repeated mechanically, "There are few worse things in life."

The next day Maria's whim about the car must still have been in the ascendant, because, coming home in the trolley, Raymond saw the unknown woman seated in her usual place. Once more her tranquil gaze took possession of the childish face opposite, making the circuit of the eyelids, tracing the line where the dark hair met the forehead, pausing at the glint of teeth between the lips. He remembered that he had not shaved for two days, touched his skinny jaw, and then, in an access of shyness, hid his hands beneath his cape.

She lowered her eyes, and he did not at first notice that, since he wore no suspenders, one of his socks had slipped down, revealing a patch of bare leg. Too nervous to pull it up, he changed his position. He was not, however, conscious of mental discomfort. What he had always hated in other people was their laughter, their smiles—even when suppressed. He could catch the faintest sign of a trembling at the corners of a mouth, knew only too well what it meant when somebody started to bite his lower lip. But the expression on this woman's face as she looked at him was something he had never met before, something at once intelligent yet animal. Yes, it was the face of some marvelous, impassive *beast,* incapable of laughter. He did not know that his father often teased Maria Cross about the way she had of adjusting laughter to her face like a mask, and then letting it fall again without the slightest hint of alteration in the imperturbable melancholy of her gaze.

When she got out of the trolley by the church at Talence, and there was nothing left for him to see except the faint dent in the leather of the seat which she had occupied, he felt absolutely certain that they would meet again next day. He could give no good reason for his hope, but just had faith in the event. That evening, as soon as dinner was over, he carried two jugs of boiling water to his room, and took down his hip bath from where it hung on the wall. Next morning he got up a good half hour earlier than usual, because he had made up his mind that henceforth he would shave every day.

The Courrèges' might have spent hours watching the slow

unfolding of a chestnut bud without even beginning to understand the mystery of the rising sap. Similarly, they were blissfully unaware of the miracle that was happening in their midst. As the first strokes of a spade may bring to light the fragments of a perfect statue, so the first glance from Maria Cross had revealed a new being in the grubby schoolboy. Beneath the warmth of her contemplative gaze a body, lovely, though ill cared for, had on a sudden stirred as might, in the rough bark of some forest tree, a spellbound goddess. The Courrèges' had no eyes for the wonder, because the members of a family too closely united lose the power to see one another properly. In the course of a few weeks Raymond had become a young man careful of his appearance, converted to the use of soap and water, secure in the knowledge that he could be pleasing to others, eager to attract. But to his mother he was still an unwashed schoolboy. A woman, without uttering a single word, merely by the intensity of her watching eyes, had transformed their child, molding him afresh, though they were incapable of detecting so much as a trace of this strange magic.

In the trolley car, which was no longer lit now that the days were lengthening, Raymond, at each encounter, ventured on some new gesture. He crossed his legs, displayed his clean and uncreased socks, his shoes shining like mirrors (there was a shoeshine boy at the Croix de Saint-Genès). He had no longer any reason to conceal his cuffs. He wore gloves. There came a day when he took one of them off, and the young woman could not suppress a smile at sight of the overpink nails on which a manicurist had been working hard, though, because for years he had been in the habit of biting them, it would have been better had they not as yet been allowed to draw attention to themselves. All this was but the outward sign of an inner, an invisible, resurrection. The fog that for so long had been collecting in the boy's most secret heart was thinning by degrees under the influence of that serious and still wordless gaze to which custom had already given a certain intimacy. Maybe he wasn't a monster after all; perhaps, like other young men, he could hold the attention of a woman—and, perhaps, more than her attention! In spite of their silence, the mere passage of time was weaving between them a web of contacts which no word or gesture could have strengthened. They felt that the moment was coming when, for the first time, they would speak, but Raymond did nothing to hasten its approach. Shy galley slave that he was, he found it enough that he no longer felt his chains. For the moment, all the happiness he needed lay in this feeling of his that he had become someone entirely different. Was it really true that until this unknown woman had begun to look at him he had been nothing but a dirty little brat? We are, all of us, molded and remolded by those who have loved us, and though that love may pass, we remain none the less *their* work—a work that very likely they do not recognize, and which is never exactly what they intended. No love, no friendship can ever cross the path of our destiny without leaving some mark upon it forever. The Raymond Courrèges who sat this evening in a small bar in the rue

Duphot, the man of thirty-five, would have been someone quite different if, in 19— when he was just embarking on his philosophy course, he had not seen, sitting opposite him in a trolley on his way home from school, Maria Cross.

5

IT WAS his father who first noticed the new man in Raymond. One Sunday, toward the end of that same spring, he was seated at the family table, more deeply buried in his own thoughts even than usual, so far buried, in fact, that he scarcely heard the noise which had started as the result of a dispute between his son and his son-in-law. The subject of the argument was bullfighting, a sport of which Raymond was a passionate devotee. He had come away that afternoon after seeing four bulls killed, so as not to miss the six o'clock trolley. But the sacrifice had gone unrewarded, because the unknown woman was not in her seat. He might have guessed as much, it being Sunday. And now she had made him miss two bulls. Thus was he busy with his thoughts while Lieutenant Basque was holding forth.

"I can't understand how your father comes to let you watch such an exhibition of slaughter."

Raymond's reply, "That's a bit comic, I must say: an army officer who can't stand the sight of blood!" started a real row.

The doctor suddenly became aware of what was going on.

"And what, may I ask, do you mean by that?"

"That you're just yellow."

"Yellow?—say that again!"

They were both on their feet. Every member of the family was now taking sides. Madeleine Basque cried to her husband:

"Don't answer him! He's not worth it! What does it matter what *he* says!"

The doctor begged Raymond to sit down.

"Get on with your meal, and let us have no more of this!"

The lieutenant shouted that he had been called a coward. Madame Courrèges maintained that Raymond had meant nothing of the sort. Meanwhile, they had all resumed their seats. As the result of a sort of secret connivance they one and all set about throwing water on the flames. Family feeling made them view with extreme repugnance anything that might upset the smooth running of their little circle. They were a crew embarked for life in the same ship, and an instinct of self-preservation made them careful to see to it that no one should start a fire. That was why silence now descended on the room. A light rain had been falling, but the sound of drops on the steps outside suddenly stopped, and the newly released fragrance of the garden drifted in to where they all sat saying nothing. Someone remarked hastily that it was already cooler, and another voice replied that the rain hadn't amounted to anything, and would barely lay the dust. The doctor, with a feeling of bewilderment, looked at the tall young man who was his son. He had hardly thought of him at all for some time, and now scarcely recognized him. He himself had just emerged from a long nightmare. He had been caught up in it ever since the day, now long past, when Maria Cross had failed to keep her appointment, and had left him closeted with Victor Larousselle. The Sunday now drawing to a close had been one of the most horrible days of his whole life, but at last it had given him back his freedom (or so he thought!). Salvation had come to him as the result of an overwhelming fatigue, an indescribable lassitude. His sufferings had been too much for him. All he wanted now was to turn his back on the battle, to go to ground in old age. Almost two months had elapsed between the ordeal of his profitless vigil in the "luxury and squalor" of Maria Cross's drawing room and this hideous afternoon which had witnessed his ultimate surrender. Seated at the now silent table, he once again forgot his son, letting his memory recall each separate circumstance of the hard road that he had traveled. In imagination he could see once more its every milestone.

The intolerable agony had started on the very morning after the broken appointment. Her letter of apology had struck the first note.

"It was to some extent *your* fault, my dear, good friend"—Maria had written in the missive which he had read and re-read over and over again, in the course of those two months:

> ". . . because it was the thought of you that gave me the idea of turning my back on a hateful luxury which had begun to make me feel ashamed. Not having the car any longer, I couldn't get back by our usual time. Being without it meant that I reach the cemetery later, and that

I stay there longer, because my conscience is clear. You've no idea how quiet it is there at the end of the afternoon, full of birds perched on the gravestones and singing. I felt that my baby-boy approved of what I had done, that he was satisfied with me. I feel already rewarded for my action by having been allowed to sit with all those working people in the trolley. You'll think I'm becoming too romantic, but indeed it is not so. It makes me feel happy to be there with all those poor people of whom I am so little worthy. I can't find words in which to tell you what that coming home in the trolley means to me. 'A certain person' is ready to go down on his bended knees, so anxious is he that I should take back the car which 'a certain person' gave me. But I won't. Dear, dear doctor, what does it really matter if we *don't* see one another? Your example, your teaching, is enough for me. We are so closely united that mere physical presence has no importance. As Maurice Maeterlinck has so wonderfully written—'A time will come, nor is it far off, when human souls will be aware of one another without the intervention of any physical organ.' Write to me. Your letters are all I need, dear spiritual director!

M. C.

"Ought I to go on taking the pills and the injections? I've only got three doses left. Must I buy another box?"

Even had it not so cruelly wounded him, this letter would have aroused the doctor's displeasure, so eloquent was it of self-satisfaction and the pleasure that comes of sham humility. There was no secret of the human heart to which he had not been made privy, and, as a result, his tolerance, where his fellow men were concerned, was almost unlimited. One vice, and one vice only, irritated him beyond bearing: the effort of the morally depraved to put a mask of beauty on their depravity. For him the last infirmity of the human creature lay in the ability to be dazzled by its own filth as by a diamond. Not that this sort of lie in the soul was habitual with Maria Cross. In fact, what had first charmed the doctor had been a power in her to see herself as she was, a refusal to embellish what was naturally ugly. One of her favorite themes had always been the noble example which her mother, a poor schoolmistress in a small country town, widowed while still young, had given her.

"She worked like a slave to pay my school fees, and had quite made up her mind that I should go to a teachers' college. She had the great happiness, before she died, of being present at my marriage, a happiness for which she had never dared to hope. Your son-in-law was well acquainted with my husband, who was a medical officer in his regiment. He adored me, and I was very happy with him. Left, as I was, with a child, I had scarcely enough to live on when he died, but I could have managed somehow. It wasn't sheer necessity that was my undoing, but something that is really much more hateful—the desire to cut a figure, the longing for the security that marriage gives. . . . What, now, keeps me from leaving 'him' is the fact that I am too cowardly to take up the struggle again, to work my fingers to the bone for an inadequate salary."

Often, since the time of those first confidences, the doctor had heard her deprecate herself, mercilessly pass sentence on her weaknesses. Why then had she suddenly fallen a victim to the detestable vice of self-praise? But what most hurt him in her letter was something quite different. His grievance against her came from the fact that he had lied to himself, that he dared not probe a far deeper wound, the only wound of which he could not endure the pain. Maria showed no desire to see him, could quite gaily envisage the possibility of their separation. Time and time again, while he was listening to some patient endlessly elaborating the details of his ailments, or to some floundering candidate hemming and hawing over the definition of hemoptysis, he heard an inner voice repeating that phrase of Maeterlinck's about human souls being aware of one another without the intervention of any physical organ. He must have been mad ever to have believed for a single moment that a young woman could feel the need for his bodily presence. Mad, quite mad: but then, what resource of reasoning can save us from the unendurable pain of knowing that the adored creature whose "being there" is a necessary condition of our continued existence, even of our physical existence, can resign herself with complete indifference (perhaps, actually, with a certain sensation of relief) to the prospect of never seeing us again? At such times we realize that we mean nothing to the one person who means everything to us.

During all this period the doctor made an effort to get the

better of himself. "I caught him again the other day looking at himself in the glass," said Madame Courrèges: "that means he's beginning to get worried." What sight better calculated to bring tranquillity and the apathy of complete despair than that of his own face, with all the telltale marks left upon it by fifty years of exhausting work? There was only one thing for him to do—to think of Maria only as he might have thought of someone dead and buried; to await the coming of death, and hasten it by doubling his daily dose of work—yes, to drive himself without mercy, to kill himself with work, to achieve deliverance through the opium of forced labor. But he who showed so little mercy to those of his fellow men who lived a lie was still the dupe of his own thoughts: She needs me: I must give her what I would give any sick person. He answered her letter with one of his own, in which he said that he felt it necessary to continue his treatment. She was perfectly right, he told her, to travel by trolley, but was it necessary for her to go out every day? He begged her to let him know when he should find her at home. He would so arrange matters as to be free to come at the usual hour.

A whole week passed without a further word from her. Each morning he had only to glance at the pile of prospectuses and newspapers to see that she had not written. He gave himself up to a calculation of probabilities: I posted my letter on Saturday. There is only one delivery on Sundays. She can't have got it till Monday. Assuming that she has waited two or three days before replying, it would be very extraordinary if I heard from her today. If nothing happens tomorrow it will be time enough for me to start worrying.

And then, one evening, when he came in from a particularly hard day, he found a letter.

"I regard my daily visit to the cemetery as a sacred duty. I have quite decided to make my little pilgrimage no matter what the weather. It is just when evening is falling that I seem closest to my lost angel. I have a feeling that he knows when I shall come, that he lies there waiting for me. I know it is ridiculous, but the heart has its reasons, as Pascal says. I am happy and at peace when I get into the six o'clock trolley. Have you any idea what a workers' trolley is like? But I feel no fear. I am not so very far removed from 'the people,' and though there may be an apparent gulf between us, am I not linked with them in another way? I look at all those men, and it seems to me that they are just as lonely as I am—how shall I put it?—no less uprooted, no less socially at sea. My house is more luxurious than their houses; still, it is nothing but a series of ready-furnished rooms. Nothing in it belongs to me any more than what is in theirs belongs to them. That is true even of our bodies. Why not call one day, very late, on your way home? I know that you don't like meeting Monsieur Larousselle. I'll tell him that I want to see you alone. All you need do when our interview is over is just exchange a few polite words with him. . . . You forgot to say anything about the pills and the injections. . . ."

The doctor's first instinct had been to tear the letter up, and scatter the fragments. Then he went down on his knees, gathered them all together, and scrambled to his feet again with considerable difficulty. Didn't she realize that he couldn't bear even the proximity of Larousselle? Everything about the man was hateful to him. He belonged to just the same general type as Basque. The lips that showed beneath the dyed mustache, the heavy dewlaps, the stocky figure, all proclaimed a complacency that nothing could shake. The fat thighs below the covert coat were expressive of an infinite self-satisfaction. Because he deceived Maria Cross with the lowest of the low, it was said in Bordeaux that he "just kept her for show." Scarcely anybody but the doctor knew that she was still the one great passion of his life, the secret weakness which drove him almost beside himself. The man might be a fool, but the fact remained that he had bought her, that he alone possessed her. Now that he was a widower, he would probably have married her had it not been for the existence of his son, the sole heir to the Larousselle fortune, who was being prepared for his august destiny by an army of nurses, tutors, and priests. It was unthinkable that the boy should be exposed to contact with such a woman, unthinkable that he should inherit a name degraded by a *mésalliance*.

"There's no getting away from it," Basque was fond of saying—for he was deeply attached to all that made for the greatness of his native place—"there's no getting away from it, Larousselle's out of the top drawer all right, he's a gentleman through and through, and what more can one ask?"

Maria knew that the doctor loathed Larousselle. How,

then, could she dare to make an appointment for the one time of the day when he would be sure to be brought face to face with the object of his execration? He went so far as to persuade himself that she had deliberately planned the meeting so as to get rid of him. After spending several weeks writing and tearing up a number of mad, furious letters, he finally sent her one that was both short and dry, in which he said that since she could arrange to be at home on only one afternoon, it must be because she was perfectly well and had no need of his ministrations. By return of post came four pages of excuse and protestation. She would, she said, be at home to him at whatever hour he might like to come on the next day but one, which happened to be a Sunday.

> "Monsieur Larousselle is going to a bullfight. He knows that I don't like that sort of thing. Come for tea. I shall wait for you until half-past five."

Never had the doctor received from her a letter in which the sublimities played so small a part, in which matters of health and treatment were not even mentioned. He reread it more than once, and frequently touched it as it lay in his pocket. This meeting, he felt, would be different from all that had preceded it. At last he would be able to declare his passion. But, man of science that he was, and taught by repeated experiences that his presentiments had a way of never being realized, he kept on saying to himself: No, it's *not* a presentiment . . . my attitude of expectancy is wholly logical. I wrote her a churlish letter to which she has sent a friendly answer. Therefore, it is up to me to see to it that our first words shall give to our talk a tone of frankness and intimacy. . . .

As he drove from his laboratory to the hospital, he rehearsed the coming interview; again and again asked *her* questions, again and again framed the replies he would have her make. He was one of those imaginative persons who never read novels because for them no work of fiction can ever be nearly so enthralling as the one they invent for themselves, the one in which they play the leading role. No sooner had he signed a prescription and found himself on the way downstairs from his patient's room, than he was back, once more, like a dog digging up a buried bone, with his fond imagined reveries. Sometimes he felt ashamed of yielding to them, but they served his ordinarily timid nature as a means of bending things and people to the all-powerful will he would have liked to possess. Scrupulous though he was in daily life, he knew no inhibitions of any kind in these adventures of the mind. He would gladly have countenanced the most appalling massacres, would even, in imagination, have blotted out every member of his family, if by so doing he could have created for himself a new and different existence.

During the two days that elapsed before his meeting with Maria Cross he did not, it is true, have to suppress any fancies of this bloodcurdling kind, but that was because in the particular episode which he had invented for his pleasure it was unnecessary to wipe out anybody. All he had to do was to break with his wife, as he had seen many of his colleagues do with theirs, and for no better reason than that he found the thought of living any longer with her unutterably boring. At fifty-two a man may still hope for a few more years of happiness, even though they may be poisoned by feelings of remorse. But why should one who has never known happiness resist a chance of tasting even its make-believe? His continued presence no longer served to bring contentment to an embittered partner, and, as to his son and daughter, well, he had long ago given up all hopes of waking any feelings of affection in *them*. Ever since Madeleine had got herself engaged he had known only too well what the love of his children amounted to. . . . And Raymond? Surely when a person is so inaccessible there is no reason why one should sacrifice oneself in vain efforts to make contact?

He realized well enough that the imagined delights in which he was now indulging were altogether different from his habitual daydreams. Even when, at a single imagined blow, he blotted out, in fancy, a whole family, he could still feel faintly ashamed, though not at all remorseful. What he was really conscious of on those occasions was a faint sense that he was making himself ridiculous. Such fantasies were purely superficial and did not involve the depths of his being. No, it had never occurred to him that he might be looked upon as a monster, or that he was in any way different from other men who, in his view, were all of them mad as soon as they were alone with their thoughts and freed from the control of others.

But, during the whole of the forty-eight hours which had got to be lived through until the appointed Sunday arrived, he knew he was clinging with all the strength that was in him to a dream that was rapidly becoming a hope. So obsessed was he by the anticipated interview with this woman that he could think of nothing but the words he had decided must pass between them. He occupied himself with putting the finishing touches to a scenario, the central situation of which could be summed up in the following piece of dialogue:

"We are both of us, Maria, at a dead end. There is only one alternative before us. Either we must die with our backs to the wall, or we must retrace our steps and—live. I know you can't love me, because you have never loved anybody. There is nothing for you to do but put yourself wholly into the hands of the one man capable of demanding nothing in exchange for his own devotion."

At this point he could hear in imagination the sort of protest she would make:

"You must be mad! What about your wife, your children?"

"They don't need me. When a man is buried alive he has the right, if he has the strength, to lift the stone that is choking him. You can have no idea of the desert that lies between me and my wife, between me and my son and daughter. The words I speak to them scarcely reach their ears. Animals, when their young have become full-grown, drive them out. More often than not the males do not even recognize them as their own. It is only human beings who invent sentiments which survive the activities of function. Christ knew this well when He said that those who followed Him must leave father and mother for His sake, who gloried in the knowledge that He had been sent to separate husband from wife, and children from those who had brought them into the world."

"You can't compare yourself to God."

"Am I not God's image in your eyes? Is it not to me that you owe your taste for a certain kind of perfection?" (But here the doctor would break off: Better keep metaphysics out of it.)

"But what about your position, your patients, the career of beneficent activity which you have built up? Think of the scandal. . . ."

"If I were to die they would have to do without me. No one is indispensable. And when I say die, I mean die, Maria. For I shall set the equivalent of death between me and the wretched hermit existence, so full of grinding labor, which I have been leading. With you I shall be reborn. What money belongs to my wife she shall keep. I can make enough for our needs. I have been offered a professorship in Algiers, another in Santiago. . . . I will hand over to my children what I have managed to save up to date."

The imagined scene had reached this point when the carriage stopped at the hospital. With his thoughts still far away, the doctor passed through the door. His eyes were the eyes of a man who is just emerging from some mysterious enchantment. As soon as his rounds were finished he returned to his daydreaming, driven on by a secret hunger, saying to himself: I am quite mad . . . all the same. . . . Among his colleagues there were men, he realized, who had made dreams like that come true. To be sure, their undisciplined lives had done something to prepare public opinion for the scandal of their break with the proprieties, whereas it was the opinion of the whole town that Doctor Courrèges was a saint. But what of that? It was just because he had got this reputation without wanting it that it would be such a relief to shed the tiresome load. Once free of it, he would no longer have to spend his time urging Maria Cross to act nobly, or in giving her edifying lectures. He would be a man with a woman to love. He would be a man strong enough to take by force everything he wanted.

At last Sunday dawned. On that one day of the seven it was the doctor's custom to attend only his most important cases. He was careful not to go near the consulting room which he kept in town. It was always swarming with patients, but he used it only three days a week. He hated the ground-floor room in a building entirely given over to offices. He couldn't, he said, have written or read a line in it. As, at Lourdes, the most trivial little thank offerings find a place, so, between those four walls, he had accumulated the various gifts showered upon him by grateful "cases." He had begun by hating the "artistic" bronzes, the Austrian terra cottas, the composition cupids, the objects in porcelain, and the combined barometers and calendars. But gradually he had developed a kind of taste for the whole horrible museum, so that he was filled with joy each time that some more than usually hideous piece of "art" found its way into his hands. "Mind, nothing *old*," his patients would say to one another when discussing how best they could please Doctor Courrèges.

But on the particular Sunday which was to enshrine his meeting with Maria Cross, the meeting that was to change the whole course of his life, he had agreed to see, at three o'clock in this same consulting room, a businessman suffering from neurasthenia who could not manage to visit the doctor on any other day of the week. He had resigned himself to the necessity. At least it would provide him with an excuse for going out immediately after luncheon, and would occupy the few last moments before that fatal meeting so eagerly awaited, so deeply dreaded. He did not use the carriage, nor did he attempt to get into any of the overcrowded trolleys. Groups of human beings were festooned about their platforms, for there was to be a big football match, and it was also the day of the first bullfight of the season. The names of Albagene and Fuentes stared from great red-and-yellow bills. Though the spectacle was not due to begin until four o'clock, the gloomy Sunday streets, with their shuttered shop fronts, were already filled with crowds making their way toward the arena. The young men wore straw hats with colored bands, or hats of light gray felt which they fondly imagined had a Spanish look. They laughed in a thick cloud of cheap tobacco smoke. The cafés breathed into the street the clean smell of absinthe. He could not remember how long it was since he had last wandered aimlessly through the hurly-burly of the city with no other preoccupation than to kill time until a certain hour should strike. To be thus unemployed was a very strange experience for a man who was usually so overworked. He had lost the secret of doing nothing. He tried to think of the experiment he had recently begun, but could see nothing with his inner eye but Maria Cross lying on a sofa with a book.

Suddenly the sun stopped shining, and the walking folk turned apprehensive eyes to where a heavy cloud was creeping across the sky. Someone said that he had felt a drop of rain, but after a few moments the sun once more came out. No, the storm would not break until the last bull had been put out of its agony.

Perhaps, reflected the doctor, things would not turn out precisely as he had imagined they would. But one thing was certain, mathematically certain: he would not leave Maria Cross without making her privy to his secret. This time he would put his question. . . . Half-past two: another hour to kill before he was due at his consulting room. At the bottom of his pocket he could feel the key of his laboratory. No, if he went back there it would mean leaving again almost as soon as he had arrived. The crowd swayed as though in the grip of a blustering wind. A voice cried: "There they are!" In a procession of ancient victorias, driven by coachmen who had caught something of reflected glory for all their shabbiness, sat the glittering matadors with their *quadrillas*. It surprised the doctor that he could discern no baseness in the emaciated faces of this strange priesthood clad in red and gold, in violet and silver. Once again a cloud blotted out the sun, and they turned their thin profiles to the tarnished azure of the sky. He thrust a way through the crowd. He was walking now along narrow and deserted thoroughfares. His consulting room, when he reached it, was as cool as a cellar. Women in terra cotta and alabaster smiled down on him from columns of malachite. The ticking of a sham antique timepiece was slower than that of an imitation Delft clock which stood in the middle of the table, where a "modern-style" female, seated on a block of crystal, did duty as a paperweight. All these various figures seemed to be singing in unison the title of a revue which had stared down on him from every corner or every street—*N'y a que ça de bon!*—including the bull in bogus bronze, his muzzle resting on the back of a companion cow. With a quick glance he took in the whole motley collection. Very quietly he said: "The human race could sink no lower!" He pushed open a shutter and set a dusty sunbeam dancing. Then he began to walk up and down the room, rubbing his hands. There must be no beating about the bush, he assured himself. With my very first words I must make her realize how terribly I suffered when I made up my mind that she no longer wanted to see me. She will express surprise. I shall tell her with all the earnestness I can command that it is impossible for me any longer to live without her . . . and then, perhaps . . . perhaps . . .

He heard the sound of the bell, went to the door, and admitted his visitor. No interruption to this daydreaming would come from *him*. All *he* asked was to be allowed to talk and talk. Neurasthenics of that sort seem to demand nothing of their doctors beyond a patient hearing. This one must have endowed the members of the profession with a kind of priestly aura, so eloquent was he in pathological confession, so anxious to display the most secret wounds of his soul. The doctor was once more, in imagination, with Maria Cross: I am a man, Maria, a poor creature of flesh and blood like other men. No one can live without happiness. I have discovered that truth rather late in life, but not too late—say it is not too late—for you to throw in your lot with mine. . . . By this time his patient had stopped talking, and the doctor, with that air of noble dignity which had earned him such universal admiration, said:

"The essential thing is that you should believe in the power of your own will. If you refuse to regard yourself as a free agent, I can do nothing for you. Even the art of healing can be wrecked on the reef of a wrong mental attitude. If you persist in thinking of yourself as the helpless victim of heredity, how can you hope that I shall be able to do anything for you? Before going further I demand from you an act of faith. You must believe that it is in your power to control all those wild beasts in yourself that are not the real you at all."

The other kept on eagerly interrupting him, and all the time he was speaking, the doctor, who had risen and gone over to the window, pretended to be looking into the empty street through the half-closed shutters. It was with something amounting to horror that he noted in himself the survival of all these lying phrases which expressed nothing but a faith long dead. Just as we perceive the light given off by a star which has been cold for centuries, so those around him heard the echo of beliefs which he had ceased to hold. He came back to the table, saw that the sham Delft clock marked four o'clock, and hastily got rid of his patient.

I've got plenty of time, he told himself as he all but ran along the pavement. When he reached the Place de la Comédie he saw that the trolleys were being besieged by the crowds of people who were pouring out of the theaters. Not a cab was to be seen. He had to take his place in a queue, and kept consulting his watch. Accustomed as he was to driving everywhere, he had left himself too little time. He tried to calm his nervousness. Even putting things at their worst he would be no more than half an hour late—no unusual thing for a doctor. Maria always waited for him. Yes, but in her letter she had said "until half-past five," and it was already five! "Just you stop pushing!" exclaimed a fat and angry woman, the feather of whose hat was tickling his nose. Inside the trolley, which was packed to suffocation, he regretted that he was wearing an overcoat. He was sweating, and hated the thought of arriving with a dirty face and a strong smell.

Six o'clock had not yet struck when he got out in front of the church at Talence. At first he walked quickly, then, mad with anxiety, broke into a trot, though his heart was troubling him. A great storm cloud had darkened the sky. In this ominous light the last bull must even now be bleeding. Between the railings of the little gardens branches of dusty lilac thrust out little begging hands, craving for rain. Under the warm slow drops he ran toward the woman whom he could see already, in imagination, stretched on her sofa. She would not immediately, on his entry, raise her eyes from her open book. . . . And then, just as he reached her front door, he saw her coming out. They both stopped. She was out of breath. Like him she had been running.

There was a hint of annoyance in her voice as she said:

"I *did* say half-past five in my letter."

He took in her appearance with an observant eye.

"You're not in mourning."

She glanced down at her summer frock and replied:

"Doesn't mauve count as half-mourning?"

How different, already, everything was from what he had been imagining! Oppressed by a great weight of cowardice, he said:

"Since you had given me up, and probably have an appointment somewhere else, we had better put off our meeting to another day."

She spoke eagerly, quickly:

"With whom *should* I have an appointment? What an odd creature you are, doctor!"

She turned back toward the house, and he followed her. She let her skirt of mauve taffeta drag in the dust. When she bent her head he could see the back of her neck. She was thinking that if she had chosen Sunday for the doctor's call it was because she felt sure that the unknown boy would not be in the six o'clock trolley. All the same, beside herself with joy and hope when he did not come at the hour named, she had run down the road, just on the off-chance, saying to herself:

There is just one possibility in a thousand that he has taken his usual trolley because of me. Whatever happens, I must not let such a chance of happiness slip.—But, alas! she would never know now whether the stranger had been struck with gloom when he saw that she was not in her usual seat. The heavy rain was splashing on the front steps as she hurried up them, and she could hear behind her the old man's labored breathing. How importunate are those who do not touch our hearts, those whom we have not chosen! They are wholly external to ourselves. There is nothing about them that we want to know. Should they die, their death would mean no more to us than their lives . . . yet it is they who fill our whole existence.

They went through the dining room. She opened the drawing-room shutters and took off her hat. Then she lay down and smiled up at the doctor, who was trying desperately to pick some shreds and tatters from the words he had so carefully prepared. She said to him: "You are out of breath. I made you walk too fast."

"I am not as old as all that."

He raised his eyes, as he always did, to the mirror that hung above the sofa. What! was he even now not familiar with his own appearance? Why was it that on each occasion he felt that stab at the heart, that sense of numb misery, as though he had expected to see his own youth smiling back at him? But already he was putting the usual question: "And how are we today?" in that tone of paternal concern, with that half-serious inflection, which he always adopted when he spoke to Maria Cross. Never had she felt so well, and in telling the doctor so she felt a pleasure which to some extent compensated her for the earlier disappointment. No, today,

Sunday, the unknown boy would almost certainly not have been in the trolley. But tomorrow, yes, tomorrow he would be there: of that there could be no doubt, and already her whole being was turned toward the joy to come, the hope that, every day, was doomed to disappointment and rebirth, the hope that something fresh might occur, that the moment would come when he would speak to her.

"I see no reason why you shouldn't leave off the injections." (He saw reflected in the glass his skimpy beard and barren brow, and remembered the burning words he had prepared.)

"I'm sleeping well: I don't feel bored any longer—just think of that, doctor! And yet, somehow, I have no wish to read. I couldn't finish *Voyage de Sparte;* you'd better take it away with you."

"You still see nobody?"

"You don't really think that I should suddenly let myself get mixed up with all these men's mistresses, do you? I, who till now have always avoided them like the plague? In the whole of Bordeaux there is no one of my kind, as you must realize, nobody of whom I could make a friend."

Yes, she had said so often enough, but always, in the past, on a note of self-pity, never, as now, with peace and happiness in her voice. It was borne in on the doctor that her long and tapering flame would no longer point heavenward a flickering tongue, would no longer burn in a void, that somewhere, close to the earth, it had found, unknown to him, fuel on which to feed. He could not keep himself from saying with aggressive emphasis that though it might be true that she did not frequent the women, she nevertheless occasionally saw the men. He felt himself blushing as he realized that the conversation might, even now, take the very tone he had so ardently desired. Indeed, Maria did actually say with a smile:

"Don't tell me you are jealous, doctor! I really do believe you're going to make a scene! No, no, don't be frightened, I was only joking," she added immediately. "I know you too well."

It was obvious that she had been within an ace of laughing outright, that it had never even occurred to her that the doctor might really be capable of such weakness. A worried look came into her eyes.

"I haven't said anything to hurt you, have I?"

"Yes, you have."

But she failed entirely to understand the nature of the hurt he spoke of. She said that her feeling for him was one of veneration and respect. Hadn't he lowered himself to her level? Hadn't he sometimes deigned to raise her to his? With a movement as insincere as her words had been, she seized his hand and drew it to her lips. He snatched it away. Annoyed by the action, she got up, went over to the window, and stared out at the drenched garden. He, too, had risen. Without turning her head, she spoke:

"Wait till the shower's over."

He made no move, but stood there in the dark room. In all things a man of method, he employed the agonizing moments in rooting from his heart all desire and all hope. Everything was over, really over. From now on, nothing that had to do with this woman would ever more concern him. He had withdrawn from the battle. With his hand he made in the empty air the gesture of a man sweeping some obstacle aside.

Maria turned her head:

"It has stopped raining," she said.

Seeing that he still did not move, she hastened to add that it wasn't that she wanted to get rid of him, but wouldn't it be as well to take advantage of this momentary break? She offered him an umbrella which at first he accepted, only, a moment later, to refuse, because he had caught himself thinking, I shall have to bring it back: that will give me a chance to see her again.

He felt no pain, but only a sense of enjoyment in the tail end of the storm. His thoughts ran on about himself, or rather one part of himself. He was like a man who finds consolation for the death of a friend in the certainty that he has ceased to suffer. He had played and lost. No use crying over spilled milk. Henceforward nothing would matter to him but his work. Yesterday they had phoned him from the laboratory to say that the dog had not survived the removal of its pancreas. Would Robinson manage to find another at the Lost Dogs' Home? The trolleys swept by, crammed with an exhausted, singing crowd. But he had no objection to walking along these suburban roads filled with lilac and smelling of the real country because of the rain and the effect of the failing light. He was done with suffering, with beating, like a prisoner, against the walls of his cell. The vital force which had been his since childhood, but which the pressure of so many human creatures had led him to dissipate, he now took back, thrusting it deep, deep into himself. Complete renunciation. In spite of staring posters and gleaming trolley lines, in spite of cyclists bent double over handlebars adorned with bunches of faded lilac, the suburb merged gradually into open country, the bars gave place to inns full of mule drivers preparing to set off by moonlight. Onward through the darkness they would trundle, like so many corpses stretched out in the bottom of their wagons, their faces to the stars. On the doorsteps of houses children were playing with drowsy cockchafers. Never again would he kick against the pricks. For how long now had he been exhausting all his energies in this dreary battle? He saw himself by the light of memory sobbing (it must be almost half a century ago) beside his mother's bed on the last day of the holidays. "Aren't you ashamed of crying, you lazy little silly-billy?" she had exclaimed, not knowing that what had provoked the outburst had simply been despair at the thought of leaving her: and later . . . once more he made that sweeping gesture with his hand, as though he were clearing a space before him. Now, what have I got to do tomorrow morning? he thought, inoculating himself, as with an injection of morphine, with the thought of daily duties . . . of the dead dog, of the need to start the whole business over again from the beginning. Surely he had tabulated a sufficient number of observations already to enable him to confirm his hypothesis? What a lot of time he had wasted. Through what thickets of shame he had been wandering! Convinced that the whole human race must be hanging on his every movement as he worked away in his laboratory, he had yet been willing to see day after day go by spoiled and empty. Science must be served with an undivided passion. It brooks no rival. I shall never be more than an amateur scientist, he thought. He imagined he saw fire burning in the branches and realized that it was the rising moon. He caught sight of the trees that hid from view the house which harbored that group of beings whom he had the right to call "my people." So often already he had been false to his vow, only later to renew it in his heart: From this very evening I will make Lucie happy. He hastened his pace, impatient to prove that this time he would not weaken in his resolve. He thought of their first meeting, twenty-five years before, in a garden at Arcachon—a meeting engineered by one of his colleagues. But what he saw with his inward eye was not the betrothed of that distant time, not a pale and faded photograph, but a young woman in half-mourning, wild with joy because he was late, and hurrying to a meeting with someone else . . . but with whom? He felt a sharp stab of pain, stopped dead for a moment, and then broke into a run so as to put as great a distance as possible between himself and the man whom Maria Cross loved. The action brought comfort, ignorant though he was that each step he took was bringing him closer to the unknown rival. . . . And yet it was on this very evening that, scarcely across the threshold of the room where Raymond and his brother-in-law stood at odds, he became conscious of a sudden burgeoning, a sudden rising of the spring sap, in the stranger whom he had brought into the world.

Those present had risen from the table, the children offering their foreheads for their elders absent-mindedly to kiss. This done, they went off to their rooms under an escort provided by their mother, their grandmother, and their still more ancient ancestress. Raymond moved across to the French window. The doctor was struck by the way in which he took a cigarette from his case, tapped it, and lighted it. There was a rosebud in his buttonhole, an orthodox crease in his trousers. The doctor thought: How extraordinarily like my poor father he is! Indeed, he was the living image of the surgeon who, until he was seventy, had frittered away on women the fortune he had amassed by the practice of his art. He had been the first to introduce into Bordeaux the blessings of antiseptic treatment. He had never paid the slightest attention to his son, to whom he habitually referred as "the young 'un," as though he had forgotten his name. One night a woman had brought him home. His mouth was twisted and dribbling. His watch, his notecase, and the diamond ring which he wore on his little finger were all missing. Paul thought: From him I have inherited a heart capable of passion, but not his gift of pleasing—that is a legacy reserved for his grandson.

He looked at Raymond, who was staring into the garden—at this grown man who was his son. After the day of feverish emotions just past he would have dearly loved to confide his troubles to a friendly ear, or, rather, to indulge in a burst of maudlin self-pity, to say to his child: "Why do we never have a good talk? Is it that you think I would not understand you? Is the gulf that separates father and son so unbridgeable? I have the same heart today as I had when I was twenty, and you are the flesh of my flesh. There is at least a good chance that we have in common the same set of tastes, antipathies, and temptations. . . . Which of us shall be the first to break this silence that divides us?" A man and a woman, no matter how completely estranged they may be, can at least come together in the ardor of an embrace. Even a mother may take between her hands the head of her grown-up son and kiss his hair. But a father can do no more than the doctor did when he laid his hand on Raymond's shoulder. The boy trembled and turned his head. His father averted his eyes and asked:

"Is it still raining?"

Raymond, upright upon the threshold, stretched his hand into the darkness.

"No, it's left off."

Then, without looking round, he added: "Good night," and the sound of his footsteps died away.

About the same time, Madame Courrèges was feeling completely "bowled over" because her husband had just suggested that she should take a turn with him in the garden. She said she would go in and fetch a wrap. He heard her go upstairs and then come down again with unwonted speed.

"Take my arm, Lucie: there's a cloud in front of the moon, and it's difficult to see one's way."

"But the path shows white."

She leaned rather heavily on him, and he noticed that her body still smelled the same as it had in the old days of their engagement, when they sat together on a bench in the long June evenings. The mingled scent of human flesh and summer dusk was, as it were, the very essence of their betrothal.

He asked whether she, too, had not noticed the great change that had taken place in their son. No, she said, he was still as surly, as sullen, as pigheaded as he had always been. The doctor pressed his point. Raymond, according to him, was now far less undisciplined. He seemed to have more control over himself. It showed, if in nothing else, at least in the care he was giving to his personal appearance.

"That reminds me. Julie was complaining only yesterday that he wants her to press his trousers twice a week."

"Julie must be made to see reason. Don't forget that she has known him ever since he was a baby."

"Julie is devoted to us, but there are limits even to devotion. It's all very well for Madeleine to talk: *her* maids do nothing at all. I know that Julie is difficult, but I do understand why she should feel annoyed at having to sweep the back stairs as well as the front."

A skinflint nightingale uttered three short notes. Husband and wife caught the hawthorn's scent of bitter almonds as they sauntered on. In a low voice, the doctor continued:

"Our little Raymond . . ."

"We shan't find it easy to replace Julie, and the sooner we realize that, the better. I know you'll say that she drives every cook we have out of the house, but more often than not she is in the right. . . . For instance, Léonie . . ."

With weary resignation he asked:

"Which of them was Léonie?"

"Surely you remember?—the fat one, not the last, but the woman who only stayed with us for three months. She objected to doing the dining room. But it isn't part of Julie's work."

He said: "Servants today are very different from what they used to be."

It was as though some tide in him were suddenly ebbing, and drawing back as it receded all desire in him to confide, to confess, to abandon pretense, to let his tears flow.

"We had better go in."

"Madeleine is forever saying that the cook is stubborn, but that's not Julie's fault. The woman wants us to raise her wages. They don't make as much out here as they do in town, though things are cheaper. If it wasn't for that they wouldn't stay at all."

"I'm going in."

"Already?"

She had a feeling that she had disappointed him, that she ought to have waited, to have let him do the talking.

"We don't often get a chance to talk," she murmured.

From somewhere beyond the wretched fabric of words that she had built up, from somewhere beyond the wall that her vulgarity had erected, with antlike patience, day by day, Lucie Courrèges could hear the stifled cry of a man who was buried alive, the shout of an imprisoned miner, and deep within herself, too, another voice replied to his, a sudden tenderness fluttered.

She made as though to lean her head upon her husband's shoulder, but guessed how his body would stiffen, his face take on an expression of hard remoteness. Raising her eyes toward the house, she could not resist saying:

"You've left the light on in your room!"

She regretted the words as soon as she had uttered them. He hurried on so as to be free of her, ran up the steps, and sighed with relief at finding the drawing room empty, because it meant that he could reach his study without meeting anybody. Safe there at last, he sat down at his table, kneaded his careworn face with both hands, and once more made that motion of sweeping something aside. . . . The dog's death was a nuisance. It wasn't easy to find animals for his experiments. With all the ridiculous nonsense that had been bothering him of late, he had lost something of his grip on things. I've been relying too much on Robinson, he thought. . . . He must have miscalculated the time of that last injection. . . . The only solution would be to begin again. From now on Robinson must confine his activities to taking the animals' temperature, to collecting and analyzing their urine. . . .

6

A FAILURE of the current had brought the trolleys to a standstill. They stood all along the boulevards, looking like a procession of yellow caterpillars. It had needed this incident to establish, at long last, some sort of direct contact between Raymond Courrèges and Maria Cross; not but what, on the day following the Sunday when they had not seen one another, a terrified feeling that they might never meet again had laid hold on both, with the result that each had separately decided to take the first step. But to her he was a shy schoolboy whom the slightest thing might frighten; and how, he felt, would he ever summon up enough courage to speak to a woman? Although for the first time she was wearing a light-colored dress, he sensed rather than saw her presence in the crowd, while she, for all her shortsightedness, recognized him from afar. There had been some sort of ceremony, and he was dressed in his school uniform, with the cape unfastened and hanging loose about his shoulders (in imitation of the cadets of the Naval Medical School). A few intending passengers got into the trolley and settled down to wait until it started. Others wandered away in groups. Raymond and Maria found themselves side by side at the far end, close to the platform. Without looking at him, so that he might not think she was speaking for his benefit, she said in a low voice:

"After all, I haven't very far to go. . . ."

And he, with head averted and cheeks all flame:

"It might be rather nice to walk home for once."

It was then that she brought herself to look him full in the face. Never before had she been so close to him.

"We've been traveling back together for so long that we mustn't lose the habit."

They walked a short distance in silence. Furtively she looked at his hot and scarlet face, at the tender skin of youth scraped and sore from the razor. With a boyish gesture he was hugging to his body with both arms a well-worn portfolio crammed with books, and the idea that he was little more than a child became firmly fixed in her mind. This realization produced in her a sense of uneasy shyness in which scruple, shame, and pure delight played an equal part. He, for his part, felt no less paralyzed with nervousness than when, in earlier days, he had decided that only the exercise of superhuman will power could induce him to enter a shop. Recognition of the fact that he was the taller of the two came as a staggering surprise. The lilac straw hat that she was wearing hid most of her face, but he could see her bare neck and one shoulder which had slipped free of her dress. The thought that he might not be able to find a word with which to break the silence, that he might ruin this precious moment, filled him with panic.

"You don't live very far away: I was forgetting."

"Not very far. The church at Talence is only about ten minutes' ride from the boulevards."

He took from his pocket an ink-stained handkerchief, mopped his forehead, noticed the ink, and put the handkerchief away again.

"But perhaps you've got farther to go?"

"Oh no I haven't: I get out just after passing the church—"

Then, very hurriedly, he added: "I'm young Courrèges."

"The doctor's son?"

There was an eager note in his voice as he asked:

"He's pretty well known, isn't he?"

She had raised her face, the better to see him, and he noticed that the color had gone from her cheeks. But even as the fact was borne in on him, she said:

"It really is a very small world. But you mustn't talk to him about me."

"I never talk to him about anything. Anyhow, I don't know who you are."

"That's just as well."

Once more she fixed on him a long and brooding look. The doctor's son! In that case, he must surely be just a very innocent and very pious schoolboy who would turn from her in horror as soon as he heard her name. It was impossible that he should not know about her. Young Bertrand Larousselle had been at school with him until last year. The name of Maria Cross must be a byword among the boys. Less from curiosity than sheer nervousness he pressed her to disclose it.

"You really *must* tell me your name. After all, I've told you mine."

The level light touched to flame a basket of oranges standing in the doorway of a shop. The gardens looked as though they had been daubed all over with dust. At this point a bridge crossed that very same railway line which once had been to Raymond an object of thrilling excitement because trains ran along it to Spain. Maria Cross was thinking: If I tell him who I am, I may lose him. . . . But isn't it my duty to scare him away? This inner debate was rich for her with pain and pleasure. She was quite genuinely suffering, but at the same time felt a vague satisfaction in murmuring to herself: "What a tragedy!"

"When you know who I am . . ." (she could not help thinking of the myth of Psyche, of *Lohengrin*).

His laugh was rather too boisterous. When he spoke, it was without restraint:

"Sooner or later we should have been bound to strike up an acquaintance in the trolley. You must have realized that I made a point of always taking the one that leaves at six. . . . You didn't? Oh, I say, come off it! I often get to the terminus early enough to catch the one before that leaves at a quarter to, but I always give it a miss, just so as to see you. Yesterday I actually came away from the fight after the fourth bull in order not to miss our meeting, and then you weren't there! They tell me that Fuentes was on the top of his form in the last kill. But now we've broken the ice why should I care *what* your name is? There was a time when I didn't care about anything, but from the moment I realized you were trying to catch my eye . . ."

Had anyone else been speaking, Maria would have found

such language atrociously vulgar, but in his mouth it had a delicious freshness, so that, later, each time she passed this particular spot on her journeys to and fro, she was to be reminded vividly of the sudden access of tenderness and joy that had been released in her by his schoolboy chatter.

"You can't get out of telling me your name. After all, I've only got to ask Papa. That'd be easy—the lady who always gets out of the trolley by the church at Talence."

"I'll tell it to you, but only on condition you swear never to talk about me to the doctor."

She no longer believed that the mention of her name would frighten him off, though she pretended to herself that the threat was real. Fate must decide, she thought—because, deep down, she was quite certain that she held the winning cards. Just before they reached the church she asked him to continue his journey alone—"because of the neighbors" who would recognize her and start gossiping.

"All right, but not until I know . . ."

Very hurriedly, and without looking at him, she said:

"Maria Cross."

"Maria Cross?"

She dug the point of her umbrella into the ground and added, precipitately:

"Wait until you know me . . ."

He was staring, as though dazzled by the sight of her:

"Maria Cross!"

So this was the woman whose name he had heard whispered one summer's day in the Allées de Tourny, when he and his companions were going back to school after the break.

She had just passed them in a two-horse brougham. One of the other boys with whom he was walking had said: "Really, women like that! . . ." And suddenly another memory came back into his mind. There had been a time when he was taking a course of medicated baths, which meant that he had to leave school at four o'clock. On this particular occasion he had overtaken young Bertrand Larousselle. He was striding along, his long legs encased in gaiters of undressed leather. Already, in spite of his tender years, he was a bullying and overbearing youth. The younger boy was, as a rule, accompanied by either a servant or a black-gloved priest with his coat collar turned up. Among the "juniors" Raymond enjoyed the worst reputation of all the "uppers," and, whenever the two of them met, the pure and pious Bertrand would devour the notorious "dirty beast" with his eyes. It never even occurred to him that to this same dirty beast he was himself an object of mystery. At this time Madame Victor Larousselle was still alive, and many ridiculous rumors about her were rife in town and school. Maria Cross, it was said, had set her heart on marriage, and was demanding that her lover should turn his family out of doors. Others announced as a fact that she was waiting until Madame Larousselle should have died of cancer, so that she could then be married in church. More than once Raymond had caught sight of Bertrand behind the closed windows of a car, driving with his corpselike mother. The women of the Courrèges and Basque families, speaking of her, used to say: "Poor thing! With what dignity she bears her martyrdom! If ever anybody had their purgatory here on earth, it's she! . . . If *my* husband behaved like that, I'd spit in his face and just clear out. *I* wouldn't stand it!"

On the day in question Bertrand Larousselle was quite alone. He heard behind him the whistling of the dirty beast and increased his pace. But Raymond kept on a level with him and never took his eyes off his short covert coat and cap of handsome English tweed. Everything that had to do with the younger boy fascinated him. Suddenly, Bertrand broke into a run, and a notebook slipped from his satchel. By the time he noticed his loss Raymond had already picked it up. Its owner turned back, his face pale with fear and anger. "Give it to me!" he cried: but Raymond read out in a low voice the title on the cover—"My Diary"—and sniggered.

"Young Larousselle's diary—that ought to be pretty juicy!"

"Give it to me!"

Raymond sprinted ahead, turned into the Parc Bordelais, and ran down one of the deserted paths. Behind him he could hear a miserable, breathless voice panting out, over and over again, "Give it to me! I'll tell them you took it!" But the dirty beast, hidden from view by a thick shrubbery, was engaged in mocking young Larousselle, who, by this time at the end of his tether, was lying full length on the grass and sobbing.

"Here's your lousy notebook, your precious diary. Take it, you little idiot!"

He pulled the boy to his feet, wiped his eyes, and brushed down the overcoat of English tweed. Whoever would have thought that the great bully could be so kind! The brat smiled his gratitude at Raymond, who, suddenly, could not resist putting into words a vulgar whim of curiosity:

"I say, have you ever seen her—this Maria Cross woman?"

Bertrand, scarlet to the tips of his ears, picked up his satchel and took to his heels. It never even occurred to Raymond to run after him.

Maria Cross . . . it was she now who was devouring *him* with her eyes. He had expected her to look taller, more mysterious. So this small woman in the lilac dress was actually Maria Cross. Noticing his confusion she mistook the cause.

"Please don't think . . ." she stammered. "You mustn't, really . . ."

She trembled in the presence of this judge whom she had viewed in the light of an angelic messenger. She saw no sign of the grubby thoughts of youth, did not know that spring is often the season of mud, and that this growing lad might be mostly composed of filth. She could not endure the contempt which she imagined him to be feeling, and, with a few hurried murmurs of farewell, was already beating her retreat. But he ran after her.

"Tomorrow, same time, same trolley?"

"Are you sure that's what you want?"

She made off then, but twice turned her head. He was standing where she had left him, thinking: Maria Cross's got a crush on me!—As though he could not believe his good luck, he spoke the words aloud: "Maria Cross's got a crush on me!"

He breathed in the dusk as though it contained the very essence of the universe, as though he could savor it in every nerve and fiber of his exultant body. Maria Cross had got a crush on him! Should he tell his pals? Not one of them would believe it. He could already see before him the leafy prison where the members of one single family dwelt side by side, yet no less cut off from one another than the worlds which make up the Milky Way. How inadequate, this evening, was that cage to house the stature of his pride! He skirted it, and plunged into a plantation of pines—the only one that was not fenced in. It was called the Bois de Berge. The earth on which he flung himself was warmer than a human body. The pine needles left deep imprints on the palms of his hands.

When he entered the dining room his father was cutting the pages of a journal, and saying something in reply to an observation of his wife's.

"I'm *not* reading—just looking at the titles of the articles."

No one but his grandmother seemed to have heard his "Good evening."

"So it's you, you young rascal!"

As he passed her chair, she put out her hand and drew him to her:

"You smell of resin."

"I've been in the pinewoods."

She looked him up and down with an air of knowing tolerance, murmuring an abusive epithet as though it had been an endearment:

"You little horror!"

He lapped up his soup noisily, like a dog. How insignificant all these people seemed to him! He was way up above them, soaring in the sunlight. Only with his father did he feel that he had some connection, because *he* knew Maria Cross, had been in her house, had attended her professionally, had seen her in bed, had pressed his ear to her chest, her back . . . Maria Cross! . . . Maria Cross! . . . the name choked him like a clot of blood. He could taste its warm saltiness in his mouth. The hot tide of it flooded his cheeks, broke from his control.

"I saw Maria Cross this evening."

The doctor fixed him with a stare.

"How did you recognize her?"

"I was with Papillon—he knows her by sight."

"Hullo!" exclaimed Basque; "Raymond's blushing!"

One of the little girls took up the phrase:

"Oo! Uncle Raymond's blushing!"

He made an ill-tempered movement of the shoulders. His father questioned him again, this time averting his eyes:

"Was she alone?"

At his son's reply—"Quite alone"—he returned to his occupation of cutting pages. Madame Courrèges said:

"It really is extraordinary how much more interested you are in that woman than in any other. What's so very odd, after all, in his having seen that creature in the street? In days gone by, when she was a domestic servant, you wouldn't have paid the slightest attention to her."

There was an interruption from the doctor: "My dear, she never *was* a domestic servant."

"Well, even if she had been," put in Madeleine, and there was a sharp edge to her voice, "that's nothing to be ashamed of—very much to the contrary, I should have thought!"

The maid having left the room with one of the dishes, she turned angrily on her mother:

"It almost looks as though you were deliberately trying to upset the servants and hurt their feelings! Irma has an extremely sensitive nature!"

"So I've got to handle the staff with kid gloves, now, have I? Really, no one would believe the things that go on in this house!"

"You can behave exactly as you like with your own servants: all I ask is that you shouldn't drive other people's away . . . especially when you expect them to wait at table!"

"You're not exactly tactful yourself where Julie is concerned, and you've got the reputation of never being able to keep a maid when you do get one. . . . Everyone knows that the only reason *my* servants ever give notice is because they can't get on with yours!"

At this point the maid came back and the altercation was interrupted. But as soon as she had once again returned to the pantry it was resumed in a series of whispers. Raymond studied his father with amusement. Had Maria Cross been a domestic servant, would *he* have so much as noticed her existence? Suddenly, the doctor raised his head, and, without looking at any of those present, announced:

"Maria Cross is the daughter of the woman who was principal of the St. Clair school when your beloved Monsieur Labrousse was curé there, Lucie."

"What? The harpy who used to plague the life out of him? Who preferred to stay away from Mass unless she and her girls could have the front seats in the nave? Well, I can't say I'm surprised: like mother, like daughter."

"Don't you remember," said Madame Courrèges the elder, "that story of poor Monsieur Labrousse's about how, when the Marquis de Lur-Saluces was beaten in the elections by a wretched little attorney from Bazas, she came round in the evening attended by the whole school, and stood under the presbytery windows jeering at him, and how her hands were quite black with letting off fireworks in honor of the new Deputy? . . ."

"A nice lot they were, I must say."

But the doctor did not wait to hear more. Instead of going upstairs as usual to his study, he followed Raymond into the garden.

Both father and son wanted to talk. Unknown to themselves some strong influence was forming a bond between them. It was as though they were harboring the same secret. In just such a way do initiates and conspirators recognize and seek one another. Each found in the other the one being in the world to whom he could unburden himself of his precious obsession. As two butterflies, separated by miles and miles, meet at the spot that houses the odorous female, so had they followed the convergent tracks of their desires, and alighted side by side on the invisible body of Maria Cross.

"Have you got a cigarette, Raymond? I've forgotten what tobacco tastes like. . . . Thank you. . . . What about taking a turn?"

He heard his own words with amazement. He was like a man who, having been cured by a miracle, sees the wound that he had thought healed suddenly open again. No longer ago than that morning, in his laboratory, he had been conscious of the lightness of spirit that comes to the devout penitent when he has received absolution. Seeking in his heart some trace of his recent passion, he had found none. How solemnly, and rather priggishly, he had lectured Robinson, who, ever since the spring, had been somewhat neglecting his work for a lady of the chorus.

"My dear chap, the scientist who really loves his work and is consumed with the desire to make a reputation will always regard the hours and minutes given over to sexual passion as so much time wasted."

Robinson had swept back his tousled hair, rubbed his spectacles on his acid-stained overalls, and ventured a protest:

"All the same, sir—love . . ."

"No, my boy, for the real scientist, except in brief moments of purely temporary surrender, his work must always take precedence of love. He will, if he sacrifices it, always be haunted by bitter thoughts of the noble satisfaction he might have known if only he had been faithful to his vocation."

"It certainly is true," Robinson had replied, "that most great scientists do occasionally indulge their sexual impulses, but I know scarcely any whom you would call men of really strong passions."

The doctor understood now why it was that this acquiescent attitude on the part of his disciple had brought the color to his cheeks.

Raymond had only to say, "I saw Maria Cross," for the passion he had thought dead to stir again. Alas! it was merely in a state of torpor . . . a single word could bring it back to life, provide it with the food it craved. It was already stretching its limbs, yawning and getting to its feet. If it couldn't embrace in flesh-and-blood reality the woman of its choice, it would find relief in speech. No matter what the cost, he *must* talk about Maria Cross.

Though they had been drawn together by a mutual desire to sing Maria Cross's praises, their very first words set father and son at odds. Raymond maintained that a woman of her emotional scope could not but outrage the anemic susceptibilities of the devout. What he admired in her was her boldness, her limitless ambition, the dissolute life which he imagined her to have led. The doctor, on the contrary, insisted that there was nothing of the courtesan about her, that one must not believe what people said:

"I *know* Maria Cross! I was her best friend during all that time when her little François was so desperately ill, and I still am. . . . She unburdened herself to me. . . ."

"My poor dear father, what you mean is that she pulled the wool over your eyes. . . ."

The doctor controlled himself with an effort. His reply, when it came, was given with considerable warmth:

"You're quite wrong, my boy. She confided in me with quite extraordinary humility. If it is true to say of anybody that their actions bear no resemblance to themselves, it is certainly true to say it of Maria Cross. Incurable laziness has been her undoing. Her mother, the St. Clair principal, got her to work for the entrance examination for the Sèvres Training College, but when she married an army doctor of the 144th regiment all that went by the board. The three years she spent as his wife were uneventful, and if he had lived she would have led an ordinary decent and humdrum existence. The only cause of complaint he had against her was that temperamental indolence to which I have already referred, because it meant that she didn't run his house well. He used to grumble a bit, she told me, when he came home of an evening, at finding that there was nothing for dinner but a dish of noodles heated up over a spirit lamp. Her favorite occupation was to lie in a torn dressing gown and slippers, reading all day long. People call her a courtesan, but you'd be surprised if you knew how little mere luxury means to her. Why, only a short time ago she decided to give up using the car which was Larousselle's present to her, and now she travels by trolley like anybody else. . . . What are you laughing at? I don't see anything particularly amusing about that. . . . Stop it! it's getting on my nerves. . . . When she found herself a widow with a child, you may imagine how ill-equipped for work an intellectual woman like that would feel. . . . Unfortunately, a friend of her husband's got her the post of secretary to Larousselle. She was completely innocent of any sort of scheming, but—well, though Larousselle had the reputation of being a harsh employer, he never said a word to her, though she was always late at the office and was hardly ever up to time with her work. That alone was enough to compromise her, and by the time she realized the situation it was too late to do anything about it. The others treated her as the boss's little bit, and their hostility made her position impossible. She spoke to Larousselle about it, which was just what he had been waiting for. He had a small property close to Bordeaux for which, just then, he had failed, or perhaps not wanted, to find a tenant. He suggested that she should act as caretaker until she could land another job. . . ."

"And I suppose she found the suggestion all innocent and aboveboard?"

"Not at all. Obviously, she realized perfectly well what he was after: but the poor woman was saddled with an establishment far too expensive for her straitened circumstances, and, to crown it all, the child was struck down with enteritis, and the doctor thought it essential that he should have country air. Finally, in view of the fact that she was already so deeply compromised, she just hadn't the courage to refuse such a windfall. She let herself be overpersuaded. . . ."

"You're telling *me!* . . ."

"Don't talk like that! You know nothing whatever about her. She stood out for a long time. But what was there for her to do? She couldn't prevent Larousselle from bringing his friends out to dinner. I realize that she was weak and irresponsible, that she ought to have refused to act as his hostess; but I can assure you that those famous Tuesday evenings were very far from being the hideous orgies of popular imagination. The only thing at all scandalous about them was that they occurred at a time when Madame Larousselle's health had taken a turn for the worse. I can swear that Maria had no idea that her employer's wife was in danger. 'My conscience was clear,' she told me. 'At that time I had not permitted Monsieur Larousselle so much as a kiss. There was nothing between us, absolutely nothing. What harm was there in my presiding over a tableful of fools? . . . I admit that the idea of dazzling them did go to my head. I enjoyed playing the bluestocking. I knew that my employer was proud of me. He had promised to do something for the boy.' "

"And you really swallowed all that? . . ."

What a simpleton his poor father was! But the thing that Raymond really resented was that the doctor should have diminished Maria Cross to the stature of a respectable, weak-willed little schoolteacher—and thereby reduced his sense of conquest to nothing.

"She didn't yield to Larousselle's suggestions until after his wife's death, and then only from lassitude, from a sort of despairing apathy—yes, that exactly describes it. She used the phrase herself when describing the situation—a *despairing apathy*. She had no illusions, was perfectly clearheaded. She was not taken in by his assumption of the role of inconsolable widower any more than she was by his promise of eventual marriage. She knew too much about men of his type, she told me, to be deluded. As his mistress she was a distinct asset, but things would be very different if she were his wife! I suppose you know that he sent young Bertrand to the Collège de Normandie so that he wouldn't be exposed to contact with her? In his heart of hearts he thought her no different from the common-or-garden drabs with whom he was forever deceiving her. Besides, I happen to know that their physical intimacy doesn't amount to much. I am convinced of that; you can take my word for it. He, of course, is mad about her, and he's not the sort of man to be content with having her just for show purposes, as is generally supposed in Bordeaux: but she is adamant. . . ."

"You're not going to tell me that Maria Cross is a saint?"

They could not see one another, but each could sense hostility in the other, though they kept their voices low. They had been brought together for a moment by the name of Maria Cross, and it was her name that separated them now. The man walked with head high: the youth kept his eyes fixed upon the ground and vented his ill-humor by kicking at a pine cone.

"You think me a fool, but of us two, it is you who are the innocent. If you think only ill of people, you'll never get to know them. You have stumbled on precisely the right word. I know what Maria Cross has been through, and I know that somewhere in her there are the makings of a saint . . . yes, really, a saint. . . . But you could never understand that."

"Don't make me laugh!"

"What do you know about her? You've merely been listening to gossip. I *do* know about her."

"I know what I know."

"And how much may that be?"

The doctor stopped dead in the middle of the path where the chestnut trees threw a deep shade. He gripped Raymond by the arm.

"Oh, let me alone! It's all one to me whether Maria Cross does, or does not, go to bed with Larousselle—but he's not the only pebble on her beach!"

"Liar!"

Raymond was brought up with a shock. "Oh, look

here . . ." he muttered. A suspicion had dawned in his mind, only to die out again almost at once, or rather to withdraw from his immediate consciousness. Exasperating his father might be, but he found it no more possible than did Maria to connect the idea of love with the rather neutral image of him which had been his since childhood. He had always seemed to him to be a man without passions and without sin, a man impervious to evil, incorruptible, living in a world far above the rather earthy concerns of other men. He heard the sound of his rather heavy breathing in the darkness.

The doctor made a violent effort to control his feelings. In a tone that was half-mocking and almost cheerful, he repeated:

"Yes, liar and humbug. All you want to do is to destroy my illusions. . . ."

And, since Raymond remained obstinately silent, he added:

"Go on, out with it. . . ."

"I don't know anything. . . ."

"You said just now—'I know what I know.' "

The boy replied that he had spoken without thinking. His manner was that of someone who has made up his mind to say nothing. The doctor did not press him. This son of his, so close that he could feel the warmth of his body and catch the smell he exuded as of some young and untamed animal, would never understand him.

"I shall stay out here a bit. Won't you sit down a moment, Raymond? There's a breeze getting up at last."

But his son said that he would rather go to bed. For a moment or two longer the doctor heard the sound he made as he kicked at the pine cones, then he was alone under the dense and drooping leaves—alive to all the passionate melancholy flung heavenward by the sleeping fields. With an immense effort he rose from his seat. The light was burning in his study. . . . I suppose Lucie thinks I'm still working. What a lot of time I've wasted! I'm fifty—no, fifty-three. What tittle-tattle has that Papillon boy been repeating? . . . He let his hands wander over the bark of a chestnut tree where he remembered that Madeleine and Raymond had once carved their initials, and suddenly, flinging his arms about the trunk, closed his eyes and laid his cheek against the smooth surface of the wood. Then he stood back, dusted the sleeves of his jacket, straightened his tie, and walked toward the house.

Sauntering between the vines, Raymond was still amusing himself by kicking a pine cone. With his hands stuck deep in his trouser pockets, he muttered to himself: "What a simple-minded old fool! there can't be many of his sort left!" Well, he at least would be equal to his opportunity; no one would lead *him* by the nose. He had no intention of prolonging his happiness through the dragging hours of this stifling night. The stars meant nothing to him, nor the scent of the pale acacia blooms. The assault of the summer darkness was powerless against this well-armed young male who was so sure of his strength in the splendid present, so sure of his young body, so utterly indifferent to all that it could not subdue and penetrate.

7

WORK, the one and only opium. Each morning the doctor woke, cured of his obsession, as though what had been gnawing at his heart had been cut out by the surgeon's knife. He left the house unaccompanied (in fine weather Raymond did not use the brougham). But his mind raced ahead of him. Already, in imagination, he was at work on his experiments. His passion diminished to a dull throb which made itself felt as a threat rather than an actuality. Whether it would become more than that, would wake again into active life, depended upon him, and upon him alone. Let him but touch the sore spot, and the sudden pain would make him cry out. . . . But yesterday his pet hypothesis had been brought tumbling to the ground by one single fact—or so Robinson assured him. What a triumph for X., who had accused him before the Biological Society of using faulty methods.

One of women's curses is that they can never free themselves of the enemy who preys upon their vitals. And so it happened that while the doctor, intent on his microscope, was blissfully unaware of his own wretchedness and of the world outside the walls of his laboratory, a prisoner pent within the confines of his observations, Maria Cross, lying on a sofa behind closed shutters, could think of nothing but the moment when she would see Raymond again, of that brief flame which alone brought warmth and brightness into the dreary sequence of her days. But how disappointing the moment was when it came! Almost at once they had had to give up their plan of traveling together as far as Talence church. Maria Cross went on ahead and met him in the Park, not far from the school buildings. He was less forthcoming now than he had been on the occasion of their first exchanges, and his attitude of shy mistrust did much to convince her that he really was only a callow boy, though an occasional snigger, a sudden furtive glance, should have put her on her guard. But she clung to her darling theory of his angelic purity. With infinite precautions, as though she were dealing with an untamed and still unsullied bird, she, as it were, crept closer and closer, walking on tiptoe and holding her breath. Everything about him conspired to strengthen the outlines of that false image of him which she had constructed: the cheeks so prone to blush, the schoolboy slang, the still visible traces of childhood that hung like morning mist about the strong young body. She was terrified by what she thought she had discovered in Raymond, though it had no existence in fact. The candor of his glance set her trembling, and she felt guilty of having brought into that frank gaze a hint of trouble and unease. Nothing occurred to warn her that when they were together he wanted only to run away, the better to gloat on the thought of her and to decide what line he had better take. Should he hire a room? Papillon knew an address, but it was a bit too squalid for a woman of her type. Papillon had told him that one could get rooms by the day at the Terminus. He'd have to find out about that. He had already walked up and down outside the hotel without being able to summon up courage enough to make inquiries at the desk. There might be other difficulties, too, of a physical nature. Over these he brooded until he had made mountains out of molehills.

Maria Cross was playing with the idea of asking him to her house, but of this plan she had, so far, said nothing. She was resolved not to smirch, even in thought, this child of nature, this untamed bird. In the stiffness of her drawing room, in the drowsy heat of the garden, their love would burgeon into words, and the storm within her breast would find relief in rain. Beyond this point she would not let imagination go. The extreme of her permitted indulgence was to fancy the feel of his head pressed to her body. He would be to her as a fawn domesticated by kindness . . . she would feel the warm, soft muzzle in her hand. . . . She seemed to see before her a long, long vista of caresses. They must be fond yet chaste. She would not let herself, even in imagination, dwell upon a fiercer pilgrimage of love, upon that ultimate bliss of tangled forest undergrowth into which they might plunge and be lost to all the world. . . . No, no—passion must never be allowed to sweep them to such extremes! Not for all the world would she destroy the childish innocence which filled her with such fear, such adoration. How to convey, without startling him into flight, that this very week he might take advantage of Monsieur Larousselle's absence on business in Belgium and venture into the stuffy and encumbered intimacies of her drawing room? Surely, if she put such a thought into words, he would at once suspect some evil intention? What she did not know was that he took his pleasure of her with far greater satisfaction to himself when they were not together, that she was with him in fancy wherever he went, or that he possessed her, turned from her, and possessed her, again and again, like a famished puppy.

At dinner the doctor kept his eyes upon him. He watched him greedily lapping up his soup, and saw, not his son, but a man who had said, speaking of Maria Cross, "I know what I know. . . ." What could that Papillon possibly have told him? It was no use deceiving himself. Quite obviously, someone of whom he knew nothing was monopolizing Maria's thoughts. I go on expecting her to write, he thought, when it should be perfectly clear that she doesn't want to see me ever again. And if that is true, it means, further, that she has given herself to another . . . but to whom? Impossible to sound the boy any more than I have done. If I insist on his telling me what he knows I shall merely be betraying myself. . . . At that point in his ruminations his son got up and left the room, without deigning to answer his mother, who called after him: "Where are you off to?"

"He goes into Bordeaux almost every evening now," she said. "I know that he gets the key of the gate from the gardener, and comes in at two A.M. by the scullery window. You ought to hear what he says when I question him. It's for *you* to do something about it, but you're so weak!"

The doctor could only stammer: "The wisest thing is to keep our eyes shut."

He heard Basque's voice: "If he was *my* son I'd bring him to heel soon enough. . . ."

The doctor got up from the table in his turn and went into the garden. He would have liked to cry aloud: "My torment is the only thing that has any reality for me!" No one realizes that it is a father's passions, more often than not, that alienate him from his son. He returned to the house, sat down at his worktable, opened a drawer, took out a packet of letters, and settled down to reread what Maria had written to him six months earlier:

> "Only the desire to become a better woman reconciles me to the necessity of living. . . . I care little what the world should know of my salvation, or that others should continue to point at me the finger of scorn. . . . Humbly I accept their censure."

He no longer remembered that, when he had read those words for the first time, such extravagance of virtue had filled him with despair, that the obligation to walk with her in so rarefied an air had been his martyrdom, that it was maddening to think that he was expected to show the way of salvation to the one woman with whom he would so gladly have gone to perdition. He thought how, reading this letter, Raymond would laugh; grew indignant at the fancy, and voiced a protest in a half whisper as though someone were walking at his side. "Bogus, you say? . . . bogus? . . . The trouble is that whenever she gets a pen in her hand she becomes too 'literary.' . . . But was that humility of tenderness when she sat by her dying child bogus, that acquiescence of hers in suffering, as though the mysterious heritage of faith had come down to her through all her mother's tedious rehash of Kantian principles? In the presence of that small bed beneath its load of lilies" (how isolated and alone the body of the dead child had looked, how silently it had seemed to be accusing her!) "she gave expression to her sense of guilt, beating her breast and groaning aloud that all was for the best, finding consolation in the thought that he had been too young to feel ashamed of her. . . ." But here the man of science intervened: The truth is rather more complicated. She *was* sincere in her grief, but, all the same, she got a certain amount of satisfaction out of her heroics—they gave her the excuse to strike an attitude. . . . Maria Cross had always had an appetite for situations of high romance. Hadn't she even gone so far as to play with the idea of having an interview with Madame Larousselle on her deathbed? It was only with the utmost difficulty that he had made her realize that scenes of that kind never "come off" except on the stage. She had given up the plan, but only on condition that he should undertake to plead her cause with the wife. Luckily, he had been able to assure her that she had been forgiven.

He went to the window, and, leaning out in the half-darkness, occupied his mind with analyzing the various night sounds—a continuous scraping of crickets and grasshoppers, the croaking of two frogs in a pond, the intermittent notes of a bird that probably wasn't a nightingale, the clanging of the last trolley. "I know what I know," Raymond had said. Who could it be that had caught Maria's fancy? The doctor pronounced one or two names, but at once rejected them. She had a horror of those particular men. But of whom *hadn't* she a horror? He thought: Remember what Larousselle told you in confidence that time he came to have his blood pressure tested—"Quite between ourselves, she doesn't really enjoy—you know what I mean. She puts up with it from me because, well, with me it's rather different. . . . It really was screamingly funny the first time I asked all these chaps to the house. They fluttered round her like moths. When a man introduces one to his mistress, one's first thought, isn't it? is whether one can cut him out. . . . Go ahead, my fine fellows, said I to myself . . . and, of course, nothing happened. They were all quite quietly kept in their place. No one knows less about love than Maria, and takes so little pleasure in it—and I'm speaking about what I know. She's as innocent as you make 'em, doctor, a great deal more innocent than most of the fine respectable ladies who turn up their noses at her." He had said, too: "It is because Maria is so completely unlike other women that I'm always terrified that, some time when I'm not there, she may make some absurd decision. She spends her whole day in a sort of dream, and only leaves the house to go to the cemetery. Do you think it's possible that she has been influenced by something she's read?"

It may be something she's read, thought the doctor: but, no; if it were I should have heard about it: books are my line of country. A book sometimes turns a *man's* life upside down, or so one's told, but does the same hold true of women? It's only life that really and truly affects them deeply, things of flesh and blood. A book?—he shook his head. The word book brought "buck" to his mind, and he had a sudden vision of some wild young animal rearing at Maria's approach.

Some cats in the grass set up a prolonged miaowing. A footstep sounded on the gravel: there was the noise as of a window being opened. It must be Raymond coming back. A moment later the doctor heard someone in the corridor. There was a knock at his door. It was Madeleine.

"Not in bed yet, Papa? I'm worried about Catherine. She suddenly started a nasty hacking cough. I was afraid it might be croup."

"Croup doesn't come on suddenly like that. I'll be along in a moment."

Some time later, as he was coming out of his daughter's room, he felt a pain in his left side, and stood leaning against the wall in the darkness, clutching at his heart. He did not call for help. His brain was perfectly clear, and he could catch from behind the door the sounds of a conversation that had just started between husband and wife.

"I know all about his being a good scientist, but science has made him skeptical. He no longer believes in medicines. But how can illness be cured without them?"

"He assured us it was nothing, not even a false croup."

"Don't kid yourself: if it had been one of his own patients he'd have prescribed something, but because it's one of the family he's not going to spend an unnecessary penny. There are times when it's an awful nuisance not being able to call in an outside man."

"But it's very convenient having him always on the spot, especially at night. When the poor old thing's no longer there, I shall never know what it is to sleep in peace, worrying about the children."

"You ought to have married a doctor, that's what *you* ought to have done!"

There was a sound of a laugh being quickly silenced by a kiss. The doctor felt the hand that was squeezing his heart loosen its grip. Very quietly he stole away. He turned in, found that he could not lie at full length without pain, and spent the night sitting upright on his bed. The whole world was asleep. The only sound was the fluttering of the leaves. . . . Has Maria ever known what it is to love? I know she's had crazes for people—for instance, there was that little Gaby Dubois girl, she tried to make her break with young Dupont-Gunther, but that was a romantic passion. She must have had some apostolic ancestor from whom she inherits that taste of hers for saving souls. Who was it, by the way, who told me a lot of ugly things about her, in connection with this same Gaby? . . . Can she be "one of them"? I remember other crazes of the same kind. . . . There may be a touch of it in her case. I've always noticed that an excess of romanticism . . . Dawn already!

He lowered his pillow, and with many precautions lay down in such a way that his wretched carcass suffered no hurt. In a few moments he had lost consciousness.

8

BUT WHAT am I going to say to the gardener?"

In one of the deserted paths of the Parc Bordelais Maria Cross was trying to persuade Raymond to pay her a visit at home. In her own house there would be no risk of their meeting people. She urged him to agree, and felt ashamed of doing so, felt that, in spite of herself, she was corrupting him. How was it possible not to see in the unreasoning terror of a boy who had once walked up and down in front of a shop because he didn't dare go in, the indisputable evidence of frightened innocence? With that thought in her mind she hastened to say:

"But, Raymond, you mustn't think I want . . . you mustn't start imagining. . . ."

"It'll be so awkward if I run into the gardener."

"But there *isn't* a gardener: I've told you so already. I'm living in an empty house which Monsieur Larousselle had not succeeded in renting. He has installed me there as caretaker."

Raymond burst into a guffaw of laughter:

"A lady gardener, eh?"

The young woman looked down so that he should not see her face, and stammered out:

"I *know* appearances are against me. After all, people can't be expected to know that I accepted the situation in perfect good faith. . . . François had to have country air. . . ."

Raymond was familiar with this particular refrain. Talk away, he said to himself, and broke in with:

"So I needn't worry about the gardener, but what about the servants?"

She reassured him on that point too. On Sundays she always let Justine, her only maid, go out. She was a married woman whose husband, a chauffeur, slept in the house so as to ensure there being a man about the place, which was none too well protected. The suburban road was not very safe. But on Sunday afternoons Justine and he always went out together. Raymond would merely have to enter by the front door and go through the dining room on the left. He would find the drawing room at the far end.

He dug his heel into the gravel with a thoughtful air. The creaking of a swing could be heard coming from behind a privet hedge. An old woman was hawking stale cakes and bars of chocolate done up in yellow paper. Remarking that he had had no lunch, he bought a crescent and a chocolate praline. As she watched him munching his meager meal, Maria suddenly saw with perfect clarity the inexorable nature of her destiny. The desire that had come to birth in her heart had been pure and limpid, yet her every action had the appearance of a monstrous depravity. When, in the trolley, her eyes had first found rest and refreshment in the young face opposite, there had been no trace of evil intention in her mind. Why should she have fought against a temptation that was so little suspect? A thirsty traveler has no reason to beware of the stream he happens on. I *do* want him to come to my house, she thought, but only because in the streets, on the bench of a public garden, I shall never succeed in probing his secret self. . . . But that doesn't alter the fact that, so far as appearances go, here is a young kept woman of twenty-seven luring a young boy into her web—the son of the only man who has ever believed in me and has never cast a stone. . . . A little later, after they had parted, and just before reaching the Croix de Saint-Genès, her thoughts returned to the subject: I want him to come, but with no evil design, not the least in the world. The very idea of such a thing makes me feel sick. But he doesn't trust me, and why should he? Everything I do is double-faced: to me it looks innocent enough, but to the world, hateful, abominable. Perhaps the world sees more truly than I do. . . . She spoke first one name, then another. If it were true that she was held in contempt for actions in which she had become unintentionally involved, she could remember others that she had done in secret, others of which no one knew but herself.

She pushed open the gate which, next Sunday, Raymond would unlatch for the first time, and walked up the drive which was overgrown with grass (there was no gardener). So heavily did the sky seem to sag that it was hard to believe the over-arching cloud would not burst with its own weight—it was as though the heavens had caught discouragement from a thirsty world. The leaves hung blighted from the trees. The maid had not closed the shutters, and great bluebottles were bumping against the bottom of the window frames. She had only just energy enough to throw her hat onto the piano. Her shoes left dirty marks on the sofa. There was only one thing possible to do—light a cigarette. But she was aware, too, of something no less habitual, the physical apathy that accompanied the activity of her imagination, no matter how wrought-up that might be. What an endless number of afternoons she had wasted lying just here, feeling slightly sick as the result of oversmoking! How many plans of escape, of self-betterment, she had elaborated, only to see them fall in ruins! To bring them to fruition she would have had, first, to stop lying there supine, to do something positive, to see people. . . . But even if I abandon all attempts to improve the external conditions of my life, I can at least refuse to do anything of which my conscience would disapprove, which might cause it to feel uneasy. Take, for instance, this case of young Courrèges. . . . She had quite decided that if she were about to lure him into her house it was only because she wanted to indulge that sweet and harmless sentiment which had come to her, originally, in the six o'clock trolley; that sense of comfort in another's presence, that melancholy pleasure of quite quietly letting her eyes take their fill—though here, in this room, she would taste it more intimately than had been possible in the trolley, and at greater leisure. But was that really all? When the presence of another person thrills us emotionally, our imagination leaps ahead, though we may not always realize it, opening up vistas the very vagueness of which has something about it that is not wholly innocent. She thought: Very soon

I should have grown tired merely of looking at him had it not been that I felt convinced that he would respond to my handling, that, sooner or later, we should speak to one another. . . . This room, so far as I can foresee, will witness nothing but motherly caresses and unimpassioned kisses, will hear nothing but spoken confidences. . . . Oh, come now, be honest with yourself! Admit that you *are* aware of the existence, beyond such innocuous happiness, of a whole region of the emotions, forbidden, it is true, yet open to exploration. There will be no barrier to break down. The field of action will lie open before you. You have only to work your way cautiously forward, to lose yourself in the misty distance as though by accident. . . . And afterward? Who is there to forbid you the enjoyment of this delight. . . . Don't you know that you could make the boy happy? . . . Ah, that's where you begin to be the dupe of your own appetites. . . . He is the son of Dr. Courrèges, of the saintly Dr. Courrèges. . . . *He* wouldn't admit that the case was even open to argument. You once told him jokingly that the moral law within him was as bright and shining as the starry sky above his head. . . .

She could hear the raindrops on the leaves, the tentative rumble of the storm. She closed her eyes, tried to fix her thoughts, concentrated her mind on the beloved face of the young boy whose innocence was wholly unsmirched (or that was what she wanted to believe), the boy who, at that very moment, was hurrying along in an attempt to outstrip the coming storm, and thinking: Papillon says it's always best to take the bull by the horns. With women of that kind, he says, brutality's the only thing that counts, the only thing they really like. . . . With his thoughts in turmoil he looked up at the growling heavens. Suddenly he began to run, his cape flung over his head, took a short cut, and jumped over a patch of shrubbery as nimbly as a buck. The storm was moving away, but it was still there. The very silence betrayed its presence. Maria had a sudden inspiration which she felt certain could not be misunderstood. She got up, sat down at her desk, and wrote:

"Don't come Sunday—or any other day. It is for your sake, and for your sake only, that I agree to this sacrifice. . . ."

She should have left it at that, and just signed her name. But some devilish counselor persuaded her to add a whole page more:

". . .You will have been the one and only happiness of a tormented and hopeless life. As we traveled home together all through this last winter, the sight of you brought me peace, though you did not know it. But the face that was your gift to me was but the outward and visible sign of a soul which I longed to possess. I wanted there to be nothing about you that I did not know. I wanted to provide the answer to your uncertainties, to smooth the path before your feet, to become for you someone who would be more than a mother, better than a friend. I lived in my dream of that. But it is not in my power to be other than I am. In spite of yourself, in spite of me, you would breathe the corruption with which the world has choked me."

On and on she wrote. The rain had settled in for good, and the only sound to be heard was that of falling water. The windows of all the rooms were shut. Hailstones rattled in the hearth. Maria Cross took up a book, but it was too dark to read, and, because of the storm, the electricity was not working. She sat down at the piano, and leaned forward as she played. It was as though her head were drawn by some attraction to her hands.

The next day, which was Friday, she felt vaguely pleased that the storm had broken the spell of heat, and spent the whole day in a dressing gown, reading, making music, idling. She tried to recall every word of her letter, to imagine the effect it would have on young Courrèges. On Saturday, after a close and heavy morning, the rain began again. She realized then the reason for her pleasure. The bad weather would prevent her from going out on Sunday, as she had meant to do, so that should the boy after all keep their appointment in spite of her letter, she would be there to receive him. Stepping back from the window through which she had been watching the rain splashing on the garden path, she said aloud in a firm, strong voice as though she were taking a solemn oath: "Whatever the weather, I shall go out."

But where would she go? If François were alive she would take him to the circus. It was her habit, sometimes, to go to a concert, where she would sit alone in a private box, or—and this she preferred—would take a seat in a public one. But on these occasions the audience always quickly recognized her. She could guess, from the movement of their lips, that people were talking about her. Leveled opera glasses delivered her up, at close range and utterly defenseless, to a world of enemies. A voice would say: "When all's said, women like that *do* know how to dress—but then, of course, with all that money it's not difficult; besides, they've nothing to think about *except* their bodies." Occasionally one of Monsieur Larousselle's friends would leave the Club Box and pay her a visit. Half turned toward the audience he would laugh loudly, proud of being seen in conversation with Maria Cross.

Except for the Saint-Cecelia concert she had, even during François' lifetime, given up going anywhere. This change in her habits had occurred after several women had insulted her at a music hall. The mistresses of all these various men hated her because she had never shown herself willing to be on terms of familiarity with them. The only one of them who, for a short while, had found favor in her eyes was Gaby Dubois. The girl, she had decided on the strength of a brief exchange of talk one evening at the Lion Rouge, where Larousselle had dragged her, was a "sweet creature." The champagne had had a good deal to do with Gaby's spiritual effervescence on that occasion. For a whole fortnight the two had met daily. With dogged determination Maria Cross had vainly tried to break the links that bound her new friend to her various other acquaintances. Then they had begun to see less and less of one another, and a little while later, during a matinée at the Apollo into which Maria had drifted from sheer boredom, alone as usual, and, as usual, drawing all eyes, she had heard, coming from a row of stalls just beneath the box where she was sitting, Gaby's shrill laughter. Other laughs had mingled with it, and odds and ends of insulting comment had reached her ears, though the voices had been kept low. "That tart who gives herself the airs of an Empress . . . who's always putting on a virtue act. . . ." It had seemed to Maria that all the faces in the theater were turned toward her—and the faces were the faces of wild beasts. Then the lights had gone down, all eyes had been riveted on a naked dancer, and she had slipped away.

After that she would never leave the house without her little boy François. And now, even though a year had passed since he had vanished, it was still he alone who could tempt her out, or rather, that gravestone, no longer than a child's body, though to reach it she had to walk along the special avenue in the cemetery marked "Adults." But Fate had ordained that on the way leading to the dead boy another, living boy should cross her path.

On Sunday morning there was a great wind—not one of those winds that serves to dandle the piled clouds, but a roarer from the south with the smell of the sea, and driving before it a sweep of muffled sky. The note of a solitary tit only emphasized the silence of a million other birds. There could be no question of going out in such weather, which was a nuisance: but by this time young Courrèges would have had her letter. Aware of the extent of his shyness, she felt sure that he would obey her injunction. Even had she not written he would probably never have dared to cross her threshold. She smiled to herself as she conjured up a vision of him digging his heel into the gravel of the drive, and saying to himself, with that mulish expression which she knew so well: "What about the gardener?" While she ate her solitary luncheon she could hear the storm raging round the house. The flying horses of the wind galloped madly on, and now, their task accomplished, were whinnying and snorting among the trees. No doubt from the cloven turmoil of the deep Atlantic they had brought flights of gulls seeking the sanctuary of the river, and kittiwakes that hold the air and do not settle. A livid coloring of seaweed seemed to tint the clouds of this suburban sky, a salty scud to splash the inland foliage. Leaning from her window that looked on the garden, Maria had the taste of it upon her lips. No, he would not come: how could he in such weather, even if she had not sent her letter? Had she not been sure of that she would have known an agony of apprehension that he might suddenly appear. Far, far better to feel that she was safe, to know for certain that he would not come. And yet, if expectation was wholly absent, why should she open the sideboard cupboard just to make sure that there was some port left?

At last the rain began to fall in a solid curtain shot with vagrant sunlight. She opened a book, but her eyes would not take in the sense of what she read. Patiently she went back to the top of the page, but in vain. Then, seated at the piano, she began to play, but not so loudly that she could not hear the sound made by the opening of the front door. She was overcome by dizziness, and just had time to say to herself: It's the wind, it must be the wind, and, a moment later, though the shuffle of hesitating footsteps reached her from the dining room—It's just the wind. She had not strength enough to get up from her chair. He was already in the room, awkward, embarrassed, not knowing what to do with his streaming hat. He did not dare to take a step forward, nor did she call to him, so powerless was she in the tumult of a passion that had burst its banks and was sweeping all before it, vengeful and frantic. In a moment it engulfed her, leaving no inch of body or soul unfilled, topping the peaks, drowning the roots, of her being. Nevertheless, when she did at last manage to speak, her expression was stern, her words no more than ordinary.

"Didn't you get my letter?"

He stood there dumbfounded. ("She wants to lead you up the garden," Papillon had said. "Don't let her put you where she wants you. Just stroll in on her with your hands in your pockets.") But, faced by what he took to be her anger, he hung his head like a schoolboy in disgrace. And she, tense and trembling with emotion, as though what she had caught in this stuffy trap of her overfurnished interior were a frightened fawn, could venture on no movement. He had come, though she had done everything in her power to keep him away. Therefore no remorse could poison this, her happiness. She could surrender to it wholly. To that destiny which had precipitated the boy into this room as food for her hunger, she swore that she would be worthy of the gift. Of what had she been afraid? There was nothing in her mind at this moment but love at its noblest. If that truth needed to be proved, proof lay in the tears which she checked, thinking of François. In a very few years he would have grown to be just such a boy as this. . . . She could not know that Raymond had interpreted the face she made in her effort not to cry as a sign of ill-humor, perhaps of anger.

She said: "After all, why not? You did well to come. Put your hat down on one of the chairs. It doesn't matter if it's damp; it's not the first wet hat their Genoa velvet has seen. . . . I'm sure you'd like a glass of port now, wouldn't you? Yes, of course you would."

While he was drinking she went on:

"Why did I write that letter? Honestly, I don't know. . . . Women do funny things . . . and then, of course, I knew you'd come in any case."

Raymond wiped his lips with the back of his hand.

"All the same, I nearly didn't come. I said to myself—she'll probably be out, and I shall look an awful fool."

"I hardly ever go out—since I've been in mourning. I've never talked to you about my little François, have I?"

François had come tiptoeing as though he were in very truth alive. Just so might his mother have kept him by her to break a dangerous tête-à-tête. But Raymond saw no more in her words than a trick designed to make him keep his distance, though Maria's only thought was to put him at his ease. Far from fearing him, she thought that she was an object of fear. Besides, this intrusion of the dead child was not of her contriving. The little boy had forced his presence on them. He had come as children do, when, hearing their mother's voice in the drawing room, they enter without knocking. The mere fact that he is there, she thought, proves, you poor dear, the purity of your intentions. What's worrying you? François is standing by your chair, not blushing but smiling.

"It's rather more than a year since he died, isn't it? I very well remember the day of the funeral. Mother made a scene . . ."

He broke off. He would have unsaid the words if he could have done so.

"A scene, why? Ah, yes, I understand. Even on that day there was no pity in people's hearts."

She rose, fetched an album, and laid it on Raymond's knees.

"I should like to show you his photographs. No one but your father has seen them. That's him at a month old, in my husband's arms. When they're as young as that they look like nothing on earth—except to their mothers. Look at this one, with a ball in his arms—laughing. That was taken when he was two. *This* was when we were at Salies. He was already ailing. I had to sell out some of my tiny capital to pay for our trip. But the doctor there was kindness and generosity itself. He was called Casamajor . . . that's him, holding the donkey's bridle. . . ."

As she leaned over Raymond to turn the pages, she was quite innocently pouring oil on the flames, stoking the blaze. Her breath fanned the fire within him. She could not see the look of fury on his face. There he sat, the heavy album weighing down his knees. He was breathing heavily and trembling with frustrated violence.

"Here he is at six and a half, just two months before he died. He looks much better, doesn't he? But I can't help wondering whether I didn't make him work too hard. When he was six he read everything that came his way, even books he couldn't understand. Living as he did, all the time with grownups.

"You see," she said, "he was my companion, my friend"—because, at this moment, she could make no distinction between what François had been for her in actuality and what she had hoped he might become.

"Even then he used to ask me questions. What nights of torment I went through thinking that one day I should have to explain. The only thing that consoles me now is the realization that he went without knowing . . . that he never knew . . . that now he never will know. . . ."

She was standing upright, her arms hanging at her side. Raymond dared not raise his eyes, but he could hear the rustling of her movements. Struck though he was by her words, he had an uneasy suspicion that her grief was not altogether genuine. Later, when he was walking home, he said to himself: She was playing a game, and taking herself in with it. . . . She was running the dead-child business for all it was worth. Still, there's no getting away from it, she *was* crying. . . . He was shaken in the idea he had formed of her. In his youth and inexperience he had painted for himself a picture of "bad women" that was entirely theological in character and modeled on what his masters had told him, convinced though he was that he had successfully resisted their influence. Maria Cross hemmed him in like an army ordered for battle. On her ankles tinkled the bangles of Delilah and of Judith. There was no treachery, no trickery that he would have put beyond one whose glance the saints had dreaded like the glance of death.

Maria Cross said to him: "Come and see me whenever you like: I am always here." With tears in her eyes and peace in her heart, she went with him to the door, without even fixing another day for their next meeting. When he had gone, she sat down by François' bed, carrying her sorrow like a sleeping child in her arms. The tranquillity she felt may have been the result of disappointment. She did not know that she would not always be safe. The dead cannot help the living. In vain do we invoke them from the edge of the abyss. Their silence, their absence, seem to take sides against us.

9

IT WOULD have been far better for Maria Cross if this, Raymond's first visit, had not left her with an impression of security and innocence. She was amazed that everything had gone so smoothly. I worked myself up unnecessarily, she thought. She believed her predominant feeling to be one of relief, but already she felt unhappy in the knowledge that she had let Raymond go without arranging for another meeting. She was careful now never to go out at the times he might be likely to come. So simple is the squalid game of passion that a youth can master it on his very first adventuring into love. It needed no worldly-wise counselor to persuade this one to "let her cook in her own juice."

After waiting for four days, she was in a fit state to lay all the blame for his silence on herself, thinking: I talked to him about nothing but my own troubles, and about François. It must have been terribly depressing for him. What possible interest could he take in my album? I ought to have asked him about his life. . . . I ought to have laid myself out to win his confidence. . . . He is bored with me . . . thinks me just a tedious woman. . . . What if he never comes back?

What if he never came back? To such an extent did she

worry over the possibility that it was well on the way to becoming a torment: I may wait as long as I like, he won't come. I have lost my hold on him. He's at the age when young men don't suffer bores gladly. Better face it, the whole thing is over and done with. . . . The evidence was too shattering, too terrible. He would never come back. Maria Cross had filled up the last well to be found in her desert. Nothing now but sand. The most dangerous of all things in love is the flight of one of the parties to the plot. The presence of the adored is, more often than not, an obstacle to passion. When she was with Raymond Courrèges she saw, in the first place, a young creature whose innocent heart it would be a crime to disturb. She remembered whose son he was. The last traces of childhood in his face reminded her of her own lost boy. Even in thought she could not draw near that young body save with a sense of ardent modesty. But now that he was no longer there, now that she feared she might never see him again, of what use was it any longer to mistrust the muddied waters of her heart, the dark confusion of her feelings? Now that this fruit was to be dashed from her thirsty lips, why deprive herself of the satisfaction of imagining the flavor she would never know in fact? Whom would she wrong by so doing? What reproach need she fear at sight of the headstone on which the name of François was engraved? Who was there to see her shut away in this house, without a husband, without a child, without servants? Madame Courrèges' endless lamentations about the quarrels of her domestic staff might be trivial enough, but how glad would Maria Cross have been to occupy her mind with such things? Where was there for her to go? Beyond the drowsing garden stretched the suburban roads, and further still the stone-built city where, when a storm bursts, one knows for certain that nine days of stifling heat will follow. A fierce and torpid beast seems to prowl, to growl, to crouch in a sky drained of all color. She too, pacing like a beast the garden or the empty rooms, yielded (how else could her misery find an issue?) little by little to the fascination of a hopeless love, a love that could offer nothing but the wretched happiness of a self-consuming anguish. She gave up all attempt to put out the fire—no longer suffered from aimlessness and lassitude, since she had no thoughts now for anything but the blaze. A nameless devil whispered in her ear: "You may be dying, but at least you are not bored!"

What is strange about a storm is not its tumult but the silence, the torpor which it imposes upon the world. Maria could see the leaves lying motionless against the panes of the window, almost as though painted on them. There was something human about the drooping melancholy of the trees. It was as though they were conscious of their lifelessness, their numbed and sleeping state. Her mood was one in which passion takes on the semblance of a physical presence. She scratched at the sore place in her soul: she kept the fire in her heart alive. Her love was becoming a choking contraction which, had she so wished, she could have localized in her throat, in her chest. A mere letter from Monsieur Larousselle had the power to make her shudder with disgust. As to the idea of his making approaches to her, *that* from now on would be no longer possible for her to endure. He would not be back for another fortnight—time enough in which to die. She gorged her imagination on thoughts of Raymond, on certain memories that formerly would have overwhelmed her with a sense of shame: I looked at the leather lining of his hat, where it presses against his forehead . . . seeking in it the very smell of his hair. . . . She yearned for his face, for his neck, for his hands, for all and each of them had become the incomparable signs and symbols of a secret reality which was filled to overflowing with delight. . . . How inconceivable was this new tranquillity at the heart of her despair. Sometimes the thought came to her that so long as he was alive nothing was lost; that maybe he would return. But as though there were something terrifying in the hope which such dreaming implied, she hastened to immure herself once more in an absolute renunciation, in the peace of mind that refuses to expect. There was for her a horrible pleasure in digging still deeper the gulf which separated her from the being whom she forced herself to see as pure. The inaccessible youth blazed in her firmament bright as the hunter Orion, and no less remote from her passion. I am already a woman burned up by life, she thought, a woman lost, while he has about him still the magic of childhood. His purity has set great spaces of sky between us, across which my longing refuses even to blaze a trail.

All through these days winds from the west and south drew after them great tumbled ranks of cloud, legions of grumbling vapor which, just as they were about to burst in a torrential downpour, suddenly hesitated, turned round about the charmed and toppling peaks of ether, and disappeared, leaving behind them that sudden sense of freshness which comes when somewhere rain has fallen.

In the night hours between Friday and Saturday the rain at last set in with an unbroken sound of murmuring waters. Thanks to the chloral that she had taken, Maria, at peace with all the world, breathed in the scented air which the garden wafted through the blinds to her tumbled bed. Then she fell into a dreamless sleep.

Lying there relaxed under the early morning sun, she thought with amazement of all the suffering she had been through. She must have been mad. Why had she seen everything in such gloomy colors? The boy was alive: he was merely waiting for a sign from her. The crisis past, she felt once more clearheaded, balanced, perhaps even slightly disappointed. Is that all it was? she thought. He'll come, and just to make doubly sure, I'll write. . . . I'm going to see him again. . . . At all costs she must confront her misery and the youth that caused it. She forced herself to contemplate in memory only a simple, inoffensive child, and was surprised to find that she no longer trembled at the thought of his head upon her knees. She thought: I'll write to the doctor telling him that I have made the acquaintance of his son (but she knew that she would not). Why shouldn't I? What harm are we doing? . . . In the afternoon she went into the garden with its waste of puddles. She felt really at peace, too wholly at peace, so much at peace that she was vaguely frightened. The less she felt her passion, the more she felt the threat of nothingness. Reduced in stature, her love no longer obliterated her inner emptiness. Already she was regretting that her round of the garden had lasted only a bare five minutes, and made the circuit once again, following the same paths. Then she hurried back because the grass had made her feet wet. . . . She would change into slippers, would lie down, smoke, read . . . but what? She had no book on hand that really interested her. As she approached the house she raised her eyes to the windows, and there, behind the drawing-room panes, saw Raymond. He was pressing his face to the glass, amusing himself by squashing his nose flat. Was this rising tide of feeling in her, joy? She walked up the front steps, thinking of the feet that, but a moment before, had pressed them. She pushed open the door, her eyes fixed on the latch because of the hand that had rested on it, crossed the dining room at a slower pace, composed her features.

It was Raymond's misfortune that he should have come immediately after the long train of days during which she had dreamed so exclusively of him, and suffered so much on his account. Seeing him there in the flesh, she could not fill the void between the endless agitation of her heart and the being who had caused it. She did not know that she was disappointed. That she was, her first remark soon proved:

"Have you just been to the barber?" She had never seen him look like this before, with his hair cut far too short, and shining. She touched the faint scar left above his temple by some blow.

"I got that falling off a swing when I was eight."

She looked at him, trying to bring into focus her desire, her pain, her hunger, her renunciation, and this long, lean youth who looked so like an overgrown puppy. A thousand feelings, all to do with him, surged up within her, and those of them she could retain grouped themselves, for good or ill, about the taut, congested face. But she failed to recognize the peculiar expression in his eyes that betokened the blind fury of the timid man who has decided to try his luck, of the coward who has screwed himself to the sticking point. Never to her had he looked so much like a child, and she said with an air of kindly authority what, so often, in the old days, she had said to François:

"Are you thirsty? I'll give you some red-currant syrup in a moment: but you must cool down first."

She directed him to an armchair, but he chose to sit on the sofa where she had already lain down. He protested that he wasn't a bit thirsty:

". . . and if I were, it wouldn't be for syrup."

Her legs were rather too much exposed, and she pulled down her skirt. The action provoked a compliment:

"What a pity!"

She changed her position and sat down beside him. He asked her why:

"It couldn't be that you're afraid?"

His words made Maria realize that that was precisely what she was. But afraid of what? This was Raymond Courrèges, young Courrèges, the doctor's son.

"How is your dear father?"

He shrugged his shoulders and stuck out his lower lip.

She offered him a cigarette which he refused, lit one herself, and leaned forward, her elbows on her knees:

"You told me once before that you aren't on very intimate terms with your father. That's natural enough. . . . Relations between parents and children are never easy. . . . When François used to hide his face against my knees, I always thought to myself—make the most of it, it won't always be like this."

She had misinterpreted the movement of his shoulders, the pouting of his lips. Just now he wanted to push the memory of his father into the background—not from any feeling of indifference, but, on the contrary, because the thought of the elder man had become an obsession with him since something odd that had happened two evenings before. After dinner the doctor had joined him on the path that ran between the vines, where he was smoking a solitary cigarette, and had walked beside him in silence, like a man who has something to say but does not say it. What's he after? Raymond had wondered, indulging to the full the cruel pleasure of silence—that same pleasure which he gave himself on early autumn mornings in the carriage, with the rain streaming down the windows. Mechanically, he had quickened his pace, because he saw that his father had difficulty in keeping up with him, and was lagging a little behind. Realizing suddenly that he could no longer hear the sound of his breathing, he had turned his head. He could see the vague outline of the doctor standing there motionless on the path between the vine shoots. His two hands were clutching at his chest, and he was swaying on his feet like a drunken man. He took a few paces forward, and then sat down heavily between two of the rows. Raymond dropped to his knees and raised the seemingly dead face to rest on his shoulder. Only a few inches separated them. He had looked at the closed eyes, at the cheeks that had taken on the color of dough.

"What's the matter, Papa, Papa, *dear?*"

The sound of his voice, at once beseeching and authoritative, roused the sick man as though it possessed some peculiar virtue. He tried to smile, but looked bewildered, and his words, when they came, were breathless.

"It's nothing. . . . I shall be all right. . . ."

He fixed his eyes on his son's worried face, heard in his voice the same note of tenderness that it had had when he was a boy of eight.

"Rest your head against me: haven't you got a clean handkerchief? Mine's dirty."

Very gently Raymond wiped the face in which, now, there were signs of returning life. The eyes were open, gazing at the boy's hair which the wind was lightly fluttering. Behind him was the dense foliage of a vine plant, and, further still, a yellowish sky full of growls and grumblings. It sounded as though it were emptying cartloads of stones. Leaning on his son's arm, the doctor returned to the house. The warm rain splashed their shoulders and their cheeks, but it was impossible to walk any faster. He had said to Raymond:

"It's this false angina—just as painful as the real thing. I'm suffering from a form of autointoxication. . . . I'll stay in bed for forty-eight hours on a diet of water . . . and remember, not a word about this to your granny or your mother."

But Raymond broke in on him with words of his own:

"You're not kidding me? You're *sure* it's nothing? Swear to me that it's nothing."

In a low voice, the doctor said:

"Would you mind so much, then, if I . . ."

But Raymond would not let him finish. He put his arm about the body that was shaking with its gasping efforts to draw breath, and his protest came in a sudden cry:

"What an old *idiot* you are!"

The doctor was to remember later the sweet insolence of the words, to remember it in the bad times when once again his child had turned into a stranger and an enemy . . . into someone whose heart was deaf to all appeals, who was incapable of responding. . . .

They went together into the drawing room, but the father dared not venture an embrace.

"Let's talk about something else: I didn't come here to chat about Papa . . . we've got better things to do than that . . . haven't we?"

He thrust forward a large and awkward paw, but she caught hold of it before it had attained its goal, restraining it with gentle insistence.

"No, Raymond, no. You live too close to him really to understand. Those closest to us are always the ones we know least about. . . . We reach a point at which we can't even see what lies beneath our eyes. Do you know, my relations always thought of me as ugly, because when I was a child I had a slight squint. I was amazed, when I went to school, to find that the other girls regarded me as pretty."

"That's right, tell me nice little stories about when you were at school!"

His fixed obsession made him look prematurely old. Maria dared not let go of the great hand. She could feel it growing damp, and a feeling that was almost disgust took hold of her. This was the same hand whose touch, ten minutes ago, had made her turn pale. There had been a time when merely to hold it in hers had compelled her to shut her eyes and turn away her head; and now, it was just a flabby, clammy object.

"I want to show you what the doctor's really like, and when I've made up my mind I can be as obstinate as a mule."

He stopped her by saying that he, too, could be obstinate.

"Look here, I swore that today I wouldn't be played with. . . ."

He spoke in a low voice, stumbling over his words; so low, indeed, that it was not difficult for her to pretend that she had not heard. But she increased the space between them. Then, after a moment, she got up and opened one of the windows: "It's stifling in here—just as though it hadn't rained at all! But I can still hear the storm, unless it's gunfire from Saint-Médard."

She pointed to where, above the trees, a dense, dark cloud showed a wind-tossed summit edged with sunlight. But he seized her forearm in both his hands and pushed her toward the sofa. She forced a laugh—"Let go!"—and the more she struggled, the more she laughed, to prove that this wrestling match was just a game, and that she regarded it as such. "Let me alone, you nasty little creature! . . ." The lines of laughter about her lips became a grimace. She stumbled against the divan, and saw, only a few inches away, the myriad drops of sweat on his low forehead, the blackheads on his nose. She could smell his sour breath. But the young faun strove to hold both her wrists in one hand so as to have the other free for what he wanted to do, and with one convulsive wriggle she freed herself. There was now between them the sofa, a table, and an armchair. She was rather breathless, but again forced herself to laugh.

"So you really think, my child, that you can take a woman by force?"

He did not laugh, the young male humiliated and infuriated by defeat, touched in the most sensitive part of that pride of body which was already abnormally developed in him, so that it bled. All his life he was to remember this particular moment when a woman had found him not only repellent but grotesque. No matter how often he might be victorious in days to come, no matter how many victims he might subdue and make miserable, nothing could assuage the burning smart of this first humiliation. For many years, remembering this moment, he would bite his lips till the blood came, would tear his pillow with his teeth in the watches of the night. . . .

He fought back the tears which sheer frustrated anger had brought to his eyes—never for an instant imagining that the smile on Maria's face might be no more than a mask, never for an instant understanding that she was seeking, not to hurt an oversensitive boy, but rather to keep herself from betraying by any sigh the sense of the disaster and the ruin in which she found herself involved. . . . If only he would go away! If only she could be left alone!

It was only such a short while ago that he had been struck with amazement to feel that the famous Maria Cross was actually within his reach. Again and again he had said to himself, This simple little creature is Maria Cross! He had only to stretch out his hand, and there she would be, inert, submissive to his will. He could take her when and how he chose, let her fall and then pull her to her feet again—and now, the movement of his outspread arms had sufficed to send her dizzily spinning out of reach. She was still there in the flesh, but he knew with a sure knowledge that from now on he could no more touch her than he could have touched a star. It was then that he realized how beautiful she was. Entirely occupied in thinking how to pluck and eat the fruit, without for a moment doubting that it was meant for him, he had never really looked at her. And now, all he could do was to devour her with his eyes.

She said, gently, for fear of irritating him, but with a terrible fixity of purpose: "I want to be alone. . . . Please listen to me, Raymond . . . you *must* leave me to myself. . . ." The doctor had suffered because he felt that Maria did not want to have him with her. Raymond knew an anguish still keener—the certainty which comes to us that the beloved object can no longer pretend, no longer hide the fact that it is the imperative need of her being not to see us any more, that she has rejected us and spewed us up. We realize, then, that our absence is necessary to her life, that she is on fire to forget us. She would hustle us from the room were it not that she is afraid we might resist.

She held out his hat, opened the door, flattened herself against the wall, while he, once more the adolescent youth, filled with horror of himself, wanted only to vanish, babbled idiotic excuses, was paralyzed with shame. But no sooner was he out on the road again, no sooner had the door closed behind him, than he found the words he should have thrown in the trollop's teeth. But it was too late! For years to come he was tortured by the thought that he had turned tail without so much as telling her what he thought of her.

While the boy, as he walked home, was voiding his heart of all the abuse with which he had been unable to smother Maria Cross, that young woman, having first closed the door and then the window, lay down. Somewhere beyond the trees a bird was uttering a fragmentary song that sounded like the broken mutterings of a man asleep. The suburban air echoed to the noise of trolleys and factory whistles. Drunken singing reached her from the Saturday streets. Yet, for all that, Maria Cross lay swaddled and stifled in silence—a silence that came not from without but from within, from the depths of her being, filling the empty room, invading the house, the garden, the city, the whole world. She lived at its airless center, her eyes fixed on that inner flame which, though suddenly all fuel was lacking, burned inextinguishably. Whence, then, did it derive its sustenance? She was reminded how, sometimes, at the fag end of her lonely evenings, a last flicker would sometimes start from the blackened ashes in the hearth where she had thought all life was dead. Eagerly she sought the loved face of the boy whom so often she had seen in the six o'clock trolley, and could not find it. All that had reality for her was a little tousled hooligan, driven beside himself with shyness, forcing himself to overcome his own timidity—a vision as different from the real Raymond Courrèges as had ever been that idealized portrait which had given beauty to her love. Against him on whom she had bestowed the transfigured features of divinity she raged and fumed: Did I suffer the torments of hell and the ecstasies of heaven for a grubby little urchin like that? . . . What she did not know was that it had been sufficient for her glance to fall upon this unformed boy for him to become a man whose dishonesties many women were to know to their cost, submitting to him as lover and as bully. If it were true that she had *created* him by virtue of her love, it was no less true that by scorning him she had added the last finishing touch to her work. She had let loose upon the world a young man whose mania it would be to prove to himself that he was irresistible, even though a Maria Cross had successfully resisted him. From now on, in all the amorous intrigues of his future, there would always be an element of unexpressed antagonism, a longing to wound, to extract a cry of pain from the female lying helpless at his mercy. He was to cause many tears to flow on many nameless faces, and always they would be *her* tears. Doubtless he had been born with the instincts of a beast of prey, but, had it not been for Maria Cross, their violence might have been softened by some touch of weakness.

How fathomless her disgust for this "hooligan"! Yet, the inextinguishable flame burned on within her though there was nothing now for it to feed upon. No human being would ever have the benefit of all this light, all this warmth. Where should she go? To the cemetery where François' body lay? No, no; far better to admit at once that the dead body of her son was nothing now to her but an alibi. She had been content in her visits to the child's grave only for the sake of the sweet homeward way which she had trodden with another, a living, child at her side. Hypocrite! What could she do, what could she say, before that tomb? She could but cast herself upon it as upon some doors she could not open, a woman damned to all eternity. As well might she fall upon her knees in the dusty street. . . . Little François was no more than a handful of ashes, he who once had been so full of laughter and of tears. . . . Whom did she wish to have near her? The doctor?—*that* bore?—no, not a bore. But what availed all her striving to attain perfection since it was her destiny to set her hand to nothing that did not turn awry, no matter how excellent her intentions? Many had been the glorious goals on which she had set her heart, yet in each of them only the worst part of herself had found its satisfaction. She wanted no one with her, nor yearned to find herself elsewhere than in this room with its torn curtains. Perhaps at St. Clair? St. Clair had seen her childhood. . . . She remembered the park into which she had crept as soon as the churchgoing family, so antagonistic to her mother, had gone away. Nature, it had seemed, was only waiting for their departure after the Easter holidays to break the coverings of all its shoots. The bracken grew high and rank, touching with formless, frothy green the lowest branches of the oaks. Only the pines swayed, unchanged, the same gray tops that seemed indifferent to the spring, and even for them a moment came when they, too, saw torn from their entrails the cloudy plenty of their pollen, the yellow immensity of their passion. At a turn in the path she would find, in those days, a broken doll, a handkerchief caught on a furze bush. But today she was a stranger to that world. Nothing would greet her there but the sand on which so often she had lain face downward. . . .

When Justine came to tell her that dinner was ready, she tidied her hair and sat down before her steaming plate of soup. But because nothing must stand in the way of her maid's visit to the movies with her husband, she was once again, half an hour later, alone at the drawing-room window. The fragrant lime had as yet no fragrance. Below her the rhododendrons already showed dark with coming color. The fear of nothingness, the longing for a breathing space, led her to seek some piece of wreckage to which she might cling. I yielded, she thought, to that instinct for flight which comes over all of us when confronted by a human face made ugly by exigence and hunger. I convinced myself that the young brute and the young creature whom I once adored were different persons—but they were the same, the same child, only wearing a mask. As pregnant women wear a mask of fretfulness, so men, obsessed by love, have, too, close-molded on their faces that look, so often hideous and always terrible, of the beast of prey that stirs within them. Galatea fled from what frightened her, yet lured her on. . . . I had dreamed of a long pilgrimage of kisses along which, making scarce noticeable progress, we should have passed from the regions of temperate warmth to those of enervating heat. But the young buck was too headstrong. Why did I not surrender to his fumbling urgency! In my raped and ravished body I might have found peace beyond imagining, something, perhaps, even better than peace. . . . Maybe, where human beings are concerned, there is no severing gulf that kisses will not bridge. . . . But kisses of what sort? Remembering the rictus of his grin, she gave vent to an "Ugh!" of disgust. A whole gallery of pictures forced themselves into her mind. She saw Larousselle turning from her with a muttered growl, his face suffused: "What *is* it you want? . . . You're just a lump of wood, not flesh and blood at all!"

What, if it came to that, did she want? She wandered about the deserted room, sat for a while by the window, looking out, elbow on sill and head on hand, dreamed of some mysterious, unvisited land of silence where she might have felt her love, yet not demand of it speech or sound, though the beloved would have heard it, would have understood the nature of her desire even before desire was born. The touch of hands and lips implies between two persons a physical separation. But so deeply interfused would they have been one with the other, that no grip and clasp of limbs would have been necessary, that brief encounter so quickly loosed again by shame. Shame? She seemed to hear the laugh of Gaby Dubois, the light o' love, the words that once she had spoken: "Speak for yourself, my dear . . . *that's* the only consolation I've got in the bloody awful life I lead. . . ." Whence came this feeling of disgust? Did it really mean anything at all? Was it something positive and personal? A thousand formless thoughts woke in her mind and disappeared again, like, in the empty sky above her head, the shooting stars and falling, burned-out meteors.

Is not my lot, thought Maria, the common lot of all womankind? Without husband, without children, no one, indeed, could be more lonely than herself. But was this solitude more actual or more intense than the sense of isolation from which no family life, however happy, could have saved her—the sense of being alone which comes to all of us as soon as we learn to recognize in ourselves the distinguishing marks of that accursed species, the race of lost souls whose instincts, needs, and mysterious ends we alone can interpret? A truce to such exhausting analysis! Pale though the sky might be with traces of the lingering day, with the promise of a rising moon, beneath the still leaves darkness was massing. Leaning out into the night air, drawn, almost physically absorbed, by the quietness of the vegetable world, Maria Cross yielded not so much to a desire to drink deep of the branch-encumbered air as to a temptation to lose herself in it, to feel herself dissolved and atomized, till the inner desert of her heart should become one with the emptiness of space, till the silence within her should in no way differ from the silence of the spheres.

10

MEANWHILE, Raymond Courrèges, having, as he walked the road, emptied his mind of all its foul abuse, and inwardly raging that he had not turned the flood on Maria Cross, felt an urgent need to spatter her with still more mud. Obsessed by that craving, he longed, as soon as he got home, to see his father. The doctor, true to his expressed intention, had decided to spend the next forty-eight hours in bed, eating nothing and drinking only water—to the great satisfaction of his wife and mother. The onset of his false angina was not alone in determining him to act in this manner. He was curious to observe the effect upon his own constitution of such a regimen. Robinson had already looked in to see him on the previous evening.

"I'd rather it had been Duluc," said Madame Courrèges, "but Robinson's better than nothing: after all he *is* a doctor, and knows all about testing the heart."

Robinson crept cautiously through the house, keeping close to the wall, and furtively climbed the stairs, dreading lest he find himself suddenly face to face with Madeleine, though they had never been actually engaged. The doctor, his eyes closed, his head feeling empty but his mind curiously lucid, his body free from pain beneath the light encumbrance of the sheets, and screened from the blaze of the sun, found no difficulty in following the tracks made by his thoughts. Here for a moment lost, there recovered, tangled and confused, they stretched before him, and his mind nosed its way along them as a dog might beat the bushes while his master walked, but did not shoot, amid the undergrowth. Without the slightest sense of fatigue he composed whole articles, to the last word, so that all that was left for him to do was to set them down on paper. Point by point he answered all the criticisms that had been provoked by the paper he had recently read to the Biological Society. His mother's presence was sweet to him —but so, also, was his wife's, and that was a matter to give him pause. Brought to a standstill at last, after an exhausting chase, he was ready to acquiesce now in Lucie's company. He noticed with appreciative wonder how careful his mother was to efface herself, and so avoid all risk of conflict. Without a shadow of mutual recrimination, the two women seemed content to share the prey, now that he had been torn for a few brief moments from his professional duties, from his private research, and from a passion which, for them, remained anonymous. He did not put up a struggle, but appeared to take an interest in all that they said, however trivial. His world had suddenly contracted to the dimensions of their own. He actually wanted to know whether Julie was really leaving, or whether there was a chance that she might come to terms with Madeleine's maid. The feel of a woman's hand upon his forehead, his mother's or his wife's, gave him back the sense of security which he had known in the days of his childhood ailments. It rejoiced him to know that if he was to die, he would not die in solitude. It seemed to him that death in that room, with its familiar mahogany furniture, with his wife and his mother forcing themselves to smile, would be the most normal, the simplest, occurrence in all the world; for would not the bitter taste of his last moments be disguised by them as always, in the past, had been the nasty taste of medicine? . . . Just to slip away, wrapped in the warm folds of a lie, knowing himself a dupe. . . .

A flood of light invaded the room. Raymond came in, grumbling that he couldn't see a thing. He approached the man lying in the bed. In his presence alone he could relieve himself of all the vicious hatred that he felt for Maria Cross. Already he could taste in his mouth the sour flavor of what he was about to vomit forth. The sick man said: "Give me a kiss." A great warmth of feeling was in the eyes which he turned upon his son who, two evenings ago, among the vines, had wiped his face. But the young man, coming straight from the daylight into the darkened room, could not make out his father's features very distinctly. There was a harsh note in his voice as he put a question:

"Do you remember our talk about Maria Cross?"

"Yes, what of it?"

Raymond, leaning above the supine body, as though for an embrace or a murderous blow, saw beneath him two tormented eyes fixed upon his lips. He realized that someone else, besides himself, was suffering. I have known it, he thought, ever since that evening when he called me a liar. . . . But he felt no jealousy. He was incapable of imagining his father in the role of lover: no, not jealousy, but a strange desire to cry, with which was mingled a sense of irritation and of mockery. The poor cheeks looked gray under the thinning beard, and there was a tightness in the voice that begged him to go on:

"Well, what is it you know? Don't keep me on tenterhooks: tell me!"

"I was misled, Papa; you are the only person who really knows Maria Cross. I just wanted to tell you that. Now try and get some sleep. How pale you look. Are you sure this diet is agreeing with you?"

It was with amazement that he heard his own voice saying the very reverse of what he had meant to say. He laid a hand upon the sad and arid brow—the same hand which Maria Cross had held such a short while before. The doctor found it cool, was afraid that it might be taken away.

"My opinion of Maria dates from far back. . . ."

At that moment, Madame Courrèges came back into the room. He put his finger to his lips, and Raymond noiselessly withdrew.

His mother was carrying a paraffin lamp (because in the doctor's weak state the electric light would have hurt his eyes). She put it on the table and lowered the shade. The restricted circle of illumination, the old-fashioned nature of its source, brought suddenly to light the mysterious world of rooms now vanished forever, where a night light had been wont to struggle with a thick darkness full of furniture half drowned in obscurity. The doctor loved Maria, but he could see her with detachment. He loved her as the dead must love the living. She made one with all the other loves of his life, from boyhood on. . . . Feeling his way along the pathway of this thought, he now saw that one and the same sentiment had always held him in thrall down the years. It had always been like the one that had caused him the torment from which he had only just been released. He could feel his way back along the dreary sameness of that eternal pilgrimage, could have put a name to each one of all the passionate adventures, most of which, like this one, had ended only in frustration. Yet, in those days he had been young. It wasn't, then, age alone that stood between him and Maria Cross. No more successfully at twenty-five than now could he have crossed the desert separating this woman and himself. He remembered how, just after he had left college, when he was the same age as Raymond, he had loved, yet never known a moment's hope. . . . It was the law of his nature that he could never make contact with those he loved. He had never been more conscious of that truth than in those moments of partial success when he had held in his arms the object so long desired, and found it suddenly poor and dwarfed and utterly different from what it had been in the agonies of his desire. No reason to seek in the mirror the reasons for that solitude in which he was fated to remain until his death. Other men—his father had been one such, Raymond would be another—can follow the law of their being into old age, obedient to the demands of their vocation of love. But he, even in his youth, had been obedient only to the call of his predestined solitude.

The ladies having gone downstairs to dinner, he heard a

sound that came straight out of his childhood, the tinkle of spoons on china. But closer to his ears and to his heart were the noises made by rustling leaves, by the crickets, by a frog pleased at the coming of the rain. Then the ladies returned. They said:

"You must be feeling very weak."

"I certainly couldn't stand upright."

But because this diet of his was a form of "treatment" they were pleased that he felt weak.

"Wouldn't you like a little . . . ?"

The sense of weakness helped him on his way of exploration into the distant past. The two ladies were carrying on a conversation in undertones. The doctor heard a name mentioned, and questioned them:

"Wasn't that a certain Mademoiselle Malichecq?"

"So you heard what we were saying? I thought you were asleep. No, it's her sister-in-law who's a Malichecq. . . . She's a Martin."

The doctor had gone to sleep by the time the Basques put in an appearance, and did not open his eyes until he heard the doors of their rooms shut. Then his mother rolled up her knitting, rose heavily from her chair, and kissed him on the forehead, the eyes, and the neck.

"Your skin's quite cool," she said.

He was alone with Madame Courrèges, who at once embarked upon a grievance:

"Raymond took the last trolley into Bordeaux again. God knows what time he'll come in. He looked terrible this evening; I felt quite frightened. When he's spent the money you gave him, he'll run into debt, if he hasn't started already!"

In a low voice the doctor said: "Our little Raymond . . . nineteen already," and shuddered, thinking of certain streets in Bordeaux that were always deserted after dark. He remembered the sailor over whose body he had tripped one evening. The man's face and chest had been blotched with stains of wine and blood. . . . Somebody was still moving about upstairs. A dog in the stable yard started to bark furiously. Madame Courrèges listened intently:

"I can hear somebody moving about. It can't be Raymond as early as this. Besides, if it were, the dog wouldn't be making all that noise."

Somebody was coming toward the house. There was nothing furtive about his movements, indeed, he seemed to be going out of his way to avoid concealment. The shutters of the French window were shaken. Madame Courrèges leaned forward.

"Who's there?"

"An urgent message for the doctor."

"The doctor doesn't go out at night: you ought to know that by this time. Try Doctor Larue in the village."

The man, who was holding a lantern in his hand, was insistent. The doctor, who was still half asleep, cried out to his wife:

"Tell him it's useless. I didn't come to live in the country just in order to be pulled out of bed by night calls."

"It's out of the question. My husband only sees patients by appointment. He has an arrangement with Doctor Larue . . ."

"But, Madame, it's about one of his patients that I've come, a neighbor of his. . . . He'll come soon enough when he hears the name. It's Madame Cross, Madame Maria Cross. She's had a fall—on her head."

"Maria Cross? Why should you think he'd put himself out for her more than for anybody else?"

But at the sound of the name the doctor had got out of bed. He elbowed his wife aside and leaned out of the window.

"Is that you, Maraud? I didn't recognize your voice. What has happened to your mistress?"

"She's had a fall, sir, on her head. She's delirious and asking for the doctor."

"I'll be with you in five minutes; just give me time to get something on."

He shut the window and started looking for his clothes.

"You're not really going?"

He made no reply but muttered to himself: "Where are my socks?" His wife protested. Hadn't he just said he wouldn't be disturbed at night for anybody? Why this sudden change of mind? He could scarcely stand up: he would faint from sheer weakness.

"It's one of my patients. Surely you see that I can't *not* go?"

There was sarcasm in her voice as she answered:

"Oh yes, I see right enough. . . . It has taken me some time, but I see now."

She did not yet actually suspect her husband. For the moment she was intent only on wounding him. He, confident in his detachment, in the fact of his renunciation, had no qualms on her account. After the long torment of his passion, nothing, he felt, could be less blameworthy, less guilty than his feeling now of friendly alarm. It never occurred to him that though he might, his wife could not draw a comparison between the past and present states of his love for Maria Cross. Two months earlier he would not have dared to show his anxiety so openly. When passion is a flaming fire we instinctively dissimulate. But once we have given up all hope of happiness, once we have accepted an eternal hunger, an eternal thirst, the least we can do—or so we think—is not to wear ourselves out with pretending.

"My poor Lucie, you're quite wrong. All that is very far away now . . . quite, quite finished. Yes, I *am* deeply attached to the poor creature . . . but that has nothing to do . . ."

He leaned against the bed, murmuring: "She's right; I've eaten nothing," and proceeded to ask his wife to make him some chocolate on the spirit lamp.

"Where do you think I'm going to find milk at this time of night? I don't suppose there's a scrap of bread in the kitchen, either. But no doubt, when you've seen to this—this woman, she'll make you a nice little supper. It will be well worth while having been disturbed for that!"

"What a fool you are, my dear. If only you knew . . ."

She took his hand and came close:

"You said—all that's quite finished . . . all that's very far away—then there *was* something between you? What was it? I have a right to know. I won't reproach you, but I want to know."

The doctor felt so breathless that he had to make two

attempts before he could get his boots on. He muttered:

"I was speaking generally: what I said had nothing to do with Maria Cross. Look at me, Lucie . . ."

But she was busy going over in her mind the events of the past months. She had the key to it all now! Everything hung together: everything was as clear as clear. . . .

"Paul, don't go to that woman. I've never bothered you with questions . . . you must do me the justice to admit that."

He answered gently that it was not in his power to do what she asked. His duty was to his patient—she might be dying: a fall on the head might well prove fatal.

"If you keep me from going out, you will be responsible for her death!"

She loosed him, finding no more to say. As he moved away from her she began speaking to herself, stumbling over her words: "It may be all a trick . . . they may have fixed it up between them." Then she remembered that the doctor had had nothing to eat since the previous evening. Seated on a chair, she listened to the murmur of voices in the garden.

"Yes, she fell out of the window . . . it must have been an accident. She wouldn't have chosen the drawing-room one, which is on the ground floor, if she had meant to throw herself out. Quite delirious . . . complaining about her head . . . doesn't remember a thing."

Madame Courrèges heard her husband tell the man to get some ice in the village: he would find some at the inn or at the butcher's. He must get some bromide, too, at the druggist's.

"I'll go by the Bois de Berge: it'll be quicker that way than if I had the horse put in."

"You won't want the lantern, sir: it's as bright as day with this moon."

The doctor had only just passed through the small gate leading to the stable yard when he heard someone running after him. A voice panted out his Christian name. He saw that it was his wife, in her dressing gown, with her hair in plaits, ready for bed. She was too breathless to say more, but held out to him a piece of stale bread and a large bar of chocolate.

He went through the Bois de Berge. The clearings were stained with moonlight, though the full strength of the white radiance could not penetrate the leaves. But the great planet sat in throned majesty above the road, shining as though in a river bed cut for its brightness. The bread and chocolate recalled the taste of all his schoolboy snacks—the taste of happiness—at dawn, when he used to go out shooting, in the days when his feet were soaked with dew and he was seventeen. Numbed by the shock of the news, he only now began to feel the pain. Suppose Maria Cross was going to die? Who was it that had made her want to die? But had she wanted it? She could remember nothing. How completely knocked out are those victims of shock who never remember anything, who smother up in darkness the essential moment of their destiny! But he mustn't question her. The important thing for the time being was that she should work her brain as little as possible. Remember, he thought, you are only a doctor attending his patient. There can be no question of suicide. When people have made up their minds to die, they don't choose a ground-floor window. She doesn't take drugs, or not as far as I know, though it's true that there was a smell of ether in her room one evening when I was there; but she'd been suffering from headache. . . .

Beyond the area of his stifling torment, on the very edge of his consciousness, another storm was growling. When the appointed moment came, it would burst: Poor Lucie—jealous! what a wretched business . . . but time enough to think about that later. . . . Here I am. The moon makes the garden look like a stage scene. It's as puerile as a setting for *Werther*. . . . No sound of raised voices. . . . The main door was ajar. From sheer habit he went straight to the empty drawing room, then turned and climbed the stairs. Justine opened the door of the bedroom. He went across to the bed, on which Maria was lying, moaning to herself, and trying to push away the compress from her forehead. He had no eyes for her body beneath the close-clinging sheet, the body which so often he had undressed in imagination. He had no eyes for her disordered hair, nor for her arm, naked to the armpit. All that mattered was that she recognized him, that her delirium was only intermittent. She kept on saying: "What happened, doctor?—what was it?" He made a mental note: amnesia. Leaning over the naked breast whose veiled loveliness had once made him tremble, he listened to her heart, then, very gently touching her injured forehead with his finger, he traced the extent of the wound. "Does it hurt you here . . . or here . . . or here?" She complained, too, of pain in her hip. Very carefully he drew down the sheet so as to expose no more than the small bruised surface; then covered it up again. With his eyes on his watch, he felt her pulse. This body had been delivered to him for cure, not for possession. His eyes knew that they were there to observe, not to be enchanted. He gazed intently at her flesh, bringing all his intelligence to bear. The clearness of his mind barred all roads of approach to his melancholy passion.

"I'm in pain," she moaned; "I'm in such dreadful pain."

She pushed away the compress, then asked for a fresh one, which the maid proceeded to soak in the kettle. The chauffeur came in with a bucket of ice, but when the doctor tried to apply it to her head, she pushed away the rubber skullcap and, in commanding tones, insisted on a *hot* compress. To the doctor she exclaimed: "Don't be so slow: it takes you an hour to carry out my orders!"

He was extremely interested in these symptoms, which were similar to others he had noticed in cases of shock. The body lying there before him, which once had been the carnal source of all his dreams and reveries and delight, roused in him nothing but an intense curiosity, a concentrated and enhanced attention. The patient's mind was no longer wandering, but she poured forth a spate of words. He noticed with surprise that she, whose powers of speech were normally so defective that she had to make an effort, and not always a successful effort, to find the right words for what she wanted to express, had suddenly become almost eloquent. She had complete command of her vocabulary, and seemed capable of calling on technical terms at will. What a mysterious organ, he reflected, is the human brain. How extraordinary it is that it can develop its scope in this amazing way merely as the result of shock.

"I never meant to kill myself—you must believe that, doctor. I absolutely forbid you to think that such an idea ever came into my mind. I can remember nothing. The only certain thing is that what I wanted was not to die but to sleep. I've never truly longed for anything in my life but peace and quiet. If ever you hear anybody boasting that he dragged me down to the point of making me want to kill myself, I tell you you mustn't believe it. Do you understand me? I pro-hib-it anything of the sort."

"Yes, dear lady. I swear to you that nobody has ever uttered such a boast in my hearing. . . . Now, just sit up and drink this. It's only bromide: it will soothe your nerves."

"I don't need soothing. I am in a good deal of pain, but I am perfectly calm. Move the lamp farther away. There now, I've messed the sheets. But I don't care—I'll empty the drug all over the bed if I want to. . . ."

When he asked whether the pain was less acute, she replied that it was excruciating, but that it didn't come only from her injury. In an access of talkativeness she once more raised her voice and spoke in such an unbroken flow that Justine observed that Madame was talking like a book. The doctor told the woman to go and get some sleep. He would sit up with the patient, he said, until daybreak.

"What other way out is there, doctor, except sleep? I see everything so clearly now. I understand what I never understood before . . . the people we think we love . . . the passions that end so miserably . . . now, at last, I know the truth. . . ." (The compress had grown cold and she pushed it away with her hand. The damp hair clung to her forehead as though she were sweating.) "No, not passions, but one single passion. It goes on inside us, and from a casual meeting, from the eyes and lips of some perfect stranger, we build up something that we think corresponds with it. . . . Only by physical contact, by the embraces of the flesh, by, in short, the sexual act, can two persons ever really communicate. . . . But we know only too well where that road leads, and why it was traced—for the sole purpose of continuing the species, as you would put it, doctor. We choose the one path open to us, but it was never designed to lead us to our hearts' desire."

At first he had lent but half an ear to this outburst. He made no attempt to understand what she was saying. What interested him was her irrelevant talkativeness. It was, he noticed, as though the physical disturbance she had suffered had sufficed partially to bring into the open ideas that had been lying repressed in her mind.

"One's got to love the pleasure of the body, doctor. Gaby used to say—it's the only thing in the world, darling, that has never disappointed me—but, unfortunately we can't, all of us, do that. And yet it *is* the only thing that makes us forget the object of our search, forget so far that it actually becomes that object. Stupefy yourself . . . that's easier said than done."

How curious it was, thought the doctor, that she should speak of sexual pleasure precisely as Pascal had spoken of faith. In order to quiet her at all costs so that she might get some sleep, he held out some syrup in a spoon. But she pushed it away, and once again made a stain upon the sheets.

"No, I don't *want* any bromide. I shall empty it all over the bed if I like: *you* can't prevent me!"

Without the slightest subtlety of transition she went on: "Always between me and those I have longed to possess there has stretched this fetid region of swamp and mud. But they didn't understand. . . . They always thought I was calling to them because I wanted to wallow in the dirt."

Her lips moved, and the doctor thought that she was muttering names, Christian names. He leaned over her eagerly, but did not hear the one name which would have utterly destroyed his peace of mind. For a few moments he forgot that she was his patient and saw only a woman who was lying to him. In an agony of misery he murmured:

"You're just like all the others. You want one thing, and one thing only, pleasure. . . . It's the same with all of us. It's the only thing we want."

She raised her lovely arms, hid her face, uttered a long-drawn moan. In a low voice he said: "What's the matter with me? I must be mad!" He renewed the compress, poured some more syrup into a spoon, and supported the sufferer's head. Maria at last consented to drink: then, after a moment's silence:

"Yes, I too, I too. You know, doctor, how sometimes one sees the lightning and hears the thunder simultaneously—well, with me pleasure and disgust are all confused, just like the lightning and the thunder: they strike me at the same moment. There is no interval between the pleasure and the disgust."

She grew calmer and stopped speaking. The doctor sat down in an armchair and watched beside her, his mind a confusion of thoughts. He believed that she was asleep, but suddenly her voice, dreamy now and at peace, rose again:

"Someone with whom we might make contact, someone we might possess—but not in the flesh—by whom we might be possessed. . . ."

Fumblingly she pushed the damp cloth from her brow. The room was filled with the silence of the dying night. It was the hour of the deepest sleep, the hour at which the constellations change their pattern in the sky so that we no longer recognize them.

Her pulse was calm. She was sleeping like a child whose breathing is so light that one gets up to make sure that it is still alive. The blood had once more mounted to her cheeks and gave them color. Her body was no longer that of a sufferer: not now did pain divorce her from desire. How long must his poor tormented flesh keep watch beside this other flesh deadened at last to suffering? The body has its agony, thought the doctor: To the simple, Paradise lies wide open. . . . Who was it said that love was the pleasure of the poor? I might have been the man who, his day's work ended, lay down each night beside this woman. But then, she would not have been *this* woman. . . . She would have been a mother more than once. All her body would bear signs of the purpose it had served, the traces of a life spent in degrading tasks. . . . Desire would be dead: nothing would remain but a few grubby habits. . . . Dawn already! How long the servant is in coming!

He was afraid that he would never be able to walk as far as his house. He told himself it was hunger that made him weak, but he dreaded the treachery of his heart whose beats he could so clearly hear. Physical anguish had freed him from love's sickness. But already, though no sign came to warn him, the destiny of Maria Cross was imperceptibly drifting away from his own. . . . The mooring ropes are loosed, the anchor raised: the vessel moves, but as yet one does not realize that it is moving, though in another hour it will be no more than a dark stain upon the sea. He had often observed that life takes no heed of preparations. Ever since the days of his youth, the objects of his affection had, almost all of them, disappeared with dramatic suddenness, carried away by some other passion, or, with less fuss and bother, had just packed up and left town. Nothing more was ever heard of them. It is not death that tears from us those we love; rather, it keeps them safe, preserving them in all the adorable *ambiance* of youth. Death is the salt of love: it is life that brings corruption. Tomorrow the doctor would be stretched upon a sickbed, with his wife sitting beside him. Robinson would be keeping a watchful eye on Maria Cross's convalescence, and would send her to Luchon to take the waters, because his best friend had set up in practice there, and he wanted to help him with a few patients. In the autumn, Monsieur Larousselle, whose business often took him to Paris, would decide to rent a flat close to the Bois, and would suggest to Maria that she move there, because, by that time, she would have said that she would rather die than go back to the house at Talence, with its worn carpets and torn curtains, or put up any longer with the insults of the Bordeaux folk.

When the maid came into the room, even had the doctor not felt so weak that he seemed to be conscious of nothing but his weakness—even had he been full of life and vigor, no inner voice would have warned him to take his last long look at the sleeping Maria Cross. He was fated never to enter this house again, yet all he said to the maid was: "I'll look in again this evening. . . . Give her another spoonful of bromide if she seems restless." He stumbled from the room, holding to the furniture to keep himself from falling. It was the only time in his life that he had left Maria Cross without turning his head.

He hoped that the early morning air would sting his blood to activity, but he had to stop at the bottom of the steps. His teeth were chattering. So often in the past, when hastening to his love, he had crossed the garden in a few seconds, but now, as he looked at the distant gate, he wondered whether he would have strength enough to reach it. He dragged himself through the mist and was tempted to turn back. He would never be able to walk as far as the church, where, perhaps, he might find somebody to help him. Here was the gate at last, and, beyond the railings, a carriage—his carriage. Through the window he could see the face of Lucie Courrèges. She was sitting there quite motionless and as though dead. He opened the door, collapsed against his wife, leaned his head on her shoulder, and lost consciousness.

"Don't agitate yourself. Robinson has everything under control in the laboratory, and is looking after your patients. At this very moment he is at Talence, you know where. . . . Now don't talk."

From the depths of his lassitude he noticed the ladies' anxiety, heard their whispering outside his door. He believed that he was seriously ill, and attached no importance to what they said: "Just a touch of influenza, but in your anemic state that's quite bad enough." He asked to see Raymond, but Raymond was always out. "He came in while you were asleep, but didn't want to wake you." As a matter of fact, for the last three days Lieutenant Basque had been in Bordeaux hunting everywhere for the boy. They had taken no one into their confidence but a private investigator. "Whatever happens, he must never know. . . ."

At the end of six days Raymond suddenly appeared in the dining room while they were at dinner. His face looked thin and tanned by exposure. There was a bruise under his right eye where somebody had hit him. He ate as though he were famished, and even the little girls did not dare to question him. He asked his grandmother where his father was.

"He's got a touch of influenza . . . it's nothing, but we were rather worried because of the state of his heart. Robinson says that he mustn't be left alone. Your mother and I take turns at sitting with him."

Raymond said that tonight he would relieve them, and, when Basque ventured to remark, "You'd much better go to bed: if you could only see what you look like! . . ." he declared that he wasn't the slightest bit tired, and that he had been sleeping very well all the time he was away:

"There's no shortage of beds in Bordeaux."

The tone in which he made the remark made Basque lower his eyes. Later, when the doctor opened his, he saw Raymond standing beside him. He made a sign for him to come closer, and, when he did so, murmured: "You reek of cheap scent . . . I don't need anything: go to bed." But toward midnight he was roused by the sound of Raymond walking up and down. The boy had opened the window and was leaning out into the darkness. "It's stifling tonight," he grumbled. Some moths flew in. Raymond took off his jacket, vest, and collar. Then he sat down in an armchair. A few seconds later the doctor heard his regular breathing. When day came, the sick man woke before his watcher and gazed in amazement at the child sitting there, his head drooping, seemingly without life, as though sleep had killed him. The sleeve of his shirt was torn, and revealed a muscular arm that was the color of a cigar. It was tattooed with the sort of obscene design favored by sailors. The congested patch beneath his eye had obviously been caused by a fist. But there were other scars on his neck, on his shoulder, and on his chest, scars that had the form of a human mouth.

11

THE REVOLVING door of the little bar never remained still for a moment. The circle of tables pressed closer and closer on the dancing couples, beneath whose feet the leather floor covering, like the wild ass's skin, continually shrank. In the contracted space the dances were no more than vertical jerkings. The women sat jammed together on the settees and laughed when they noticed on bare arms the mark of an involuntary caress. The one called Gladys and her companion put on their fur coats.

"You staying?"

Larousselle protested that they were leaving just as things might get amusing. With his hands thrust into his pockets, unsteady on his feet, and his paunch sticking out provocatively, he went across and perched himself on a high stool. The barman burst out laughing, as did the young men to whom he was explaining with considerable pride the ingredients of a special aphrodisiac cocktail of his own invention. Maria, alone at her table, took another sip of champagne and put down her glass. She smiled vaguely, utterly indifferent to Raymond's proximity. What passion might occupy her mind he could not know. She was armed against him, separated from him, by the accumulated experiences of seventeen years. Like a dazed and blinded diver he fought his way to the surface, up from the dead past. But the only thing in the unclear backwash of time that really belonged wholly to him was a narrow path, quickly traversed, between walls of clotted darkness. With his nose to the ground he had followed the scent, oblivious to all others that might cross it. But this was no place for dreaming. Across the smoky room and the crowd of dancing couples Maria gave him a hasty glance, then turned away. Why had he not even smiled at her? He dreaded to think that after all these years the youth that once he had been might again take visionary form in this woman's eyes, that image of the shy young boy in the grip of an impotent and furtive desire. Courrèges, notorious for his audacities, trembled with anxiety this evening lest, at any moment now, Maria might get up and disappear. Wasn't there anything he could try? He was the victim of that fatality which condemns us to play the role of a man in whom a woman makes exclusive, unalterable choice of certain elements, forever ignoring those others that may, too, be part of him. There is nothing to be done against this particular chemical law. Every human being with whom we come in contact isolates in us a single property, always the same, which as a rule we should prefer to keep concealed. Our misery, on these occasions, consists in our seeing the loved one build up, beneath our very eyes, the portrait of us that she has made, reduce to nothing our most precious virtues, and turn the light full on our one weakness, absurdity, or vice. And not only that. We are forced to share in the vision, to conform to it, for just so long as those appraising eyes, with their single, fixed idea, are bent on us. Only to others, whose affection is of no value to us, will our virtues glow, our talents shine, our strength seem superhuman, our face become as the face of a god.

Now that he had become, under Maria Cross's gaze, once more an abashed and foolish youth, Courrèges no longer wanted to revenge himself. His humble desire went no further than that this woman might learn the details of his amorous career, of all the victories he had won from that moment when, shortly after he had been thrown out of the house at Talence, he had been taken up, almost kidnaped, by an American woman who had kept him for six months at the Ritz (his family believed that he was in Paris working for his exam). But it was just that, he told himself, that was so impossible—to show himself as someone totally different from what he had been in that overfurnished drawing room, all "luxury and squalor," when she had said, averting her face, "I want to be alone, Raymond—listen to me—you *must* leave me to myself."

It was the hour at which the tide begins to ebb. But those regular patrons of the little bar who left their troubles with their coats in the cloakroom stayed on. A young woman in red was whirling round ecstatically, her arms extended like wings, while her partner held her by the waist—two happy May flies united in full flight. An American showed the smooth face of a schoolboy above a pair of enormous shoulders. With ears only for the voice of some god within him, he danced alone, improvising steps which were probably obscene. To the applause which greeted his efforts he responded awkwardly with the grin of a happy child.

Victor Larousselle had resumed his seat opposite Maria. Now and again he turned his head and stared at Raymond. His large face, of a uniform alcoholic red (except under the eyes, where there were livid pouches), had the look of a man eager for a sign of recognition. In vain did Maria beg him to turn his attention elsewhere. If there was one thing above all others about Paris that Larousselle could not bear, it was seeing so many strange faces. At home there was scarcely one that did not immediately bring to mind some name, some married relationship, someone whom he could immediately "place"—whether publicly, as a person demanding social acknowledgment, or surreptitiously, as a member of the half-world whom he might know but could not openly greet. Nothing is commoner than that memory for faces which historians attribute only to the great. Larousselle remembered Raymond perfectly well from having seen him driving with his father in the old days, and from having occasionally patted his head. At Bordeaux, in the Cours de l'Intendance, he would have made no sign of recognition, but here, apart from the fact that he could never get used to the humiliation of passing forever unnoticed, he was secretly anxious that Maria should not be left alone while he played the fool with the two Russian girls who were so obviously wearing nothing under their frocks. Raymond, acutely conscious of Maria's every gesture, concluded that she was doing her best to prevent Larousselle from speaking to him. He was convinced that, even after the lapse of seventeen years, she still saw him as an uncouth and furtive oaf. He heard the man from Bordeaux snarl: "Well, I *want* to, and that ought to be enough for you!" A smile lay like a mask on his unpleasant countenance as he picked his way toward Raymond with all the self-confidence of a man who believes his handshake to be a privilege. Surely, he *couldn't* be mistaken? he said. It was, wasn't it, the son of that excellent doctor Courrèges? His wife remembered quite clearly that she had known him at the time when the doctor was attending her. . . . He was completely master of the situation, took the young man's glass, and made him sit down beside Maria, who held out her hand, and then, almost immediately, withdrew it. Larousselle, after sitting down for a few moments, jumped up again and said without the slightest show of embarrassment:

"Forgive me, will you?—back in a minute."

He joined the two young Russian women at the bar. Though it might be only a matter of moments before he would be back again, and though nothing seemed to Raymond more important than to turn this short respite to the best advantage, he remained silent. Maria turned away her head. He could smell the fragrance of her short hair, and noticed with deep emotion that a few of the strands were white. A few?—thousands perhaps! The strongly marked, rather thick lips seemed miraculously untouched by age, and still gave him the impression of fruit ripe for the picking. In them was concentrated all the sensuality of her body. The light in her eyes, under the wide, exposed brow, was astonishingly pure. What did it matter if the storms of time had beaten against, had slowly eaten away and relaxed, the lines of neck and throat?

Without looking at him, she said:

"My husband is really very indiscreet. . . ."

Raymond, as sheepish now as he could ever have been at eighteen, betrayed his amazement at the news that she was married.

"Do you mean to say you didn't know? It's common knowledge in Bordeaux."

She had made up her mind to maintain an icy silence, but seemed astounded to find that there was anybody in the world—least of all a man from Bordeaux—who was ignorant of the fact that she was now Madame Victor Larousselle. He explained that it had been many years since he'd lived in that city. At that she could no longer keep from breaking her vow of silence. Monsieur Larousselle, she said, had made up his mind the year after the war . . . he had waited until then because of his son.

"Actually, it was Bertrand who begged us, almost before he was out of the army, to get the whole thing settled. It didn't matter to me one way or the other. . . . I agreed from the highest motives only."

She added that she would have preferred to go on living in Bordeaux:

"But Bertrand is at the Polytechnic. Besides, Monsieur Larousselle has to be in Paris for a fortnight every month, so we thought it better to make a home there for the boy."

She seemed suddenly overcome by shyness at having

spoken like this, at having confided in him. Once again remote, she said:

"And the dear doctor? Life has a way of separating us from our best friends. . . ."

How delightful it would be to see him again! But when Raymond, taking her at her word, replied: "As a matter of fact, my father is in Paris at this very moment, at the Grand Hotel. He would be more than pleased . . ." she stopped short, and appeared not to have heard him.

Eager to touch her on the raw, to rouse her to a show of anger, he took his courage in both hands and proceeded to voice his one burning preoccupation:

"You don't still hold my boorishness against me? I was only a clumsy child in those days, and really very innocent. Tell me you don't bear me a grudge . . ."

"Bear a grudge?"

She pretended not to understand. Then:

"Oh, you're referring to that ridiculous scene . . . really, there's nothing to forgive. I think I must have been slightly mad myself. Fancy taking a little boy like you seriously! It all seems to me so entirely unimportant now . . . so very, very far away."

He certainly had touched her on the raw, though not in the way he had expected. She had a horror of all that reminded her of the old Maria Cross, but the adventure in which Raymond had played a part she looked on as merely ridiculous. Suddenly grown cautious, she found herself wondering whether he had ever known that she had tried to kill herself. No, for if he had he would have been prouder, would have seemed less humble.

As for Raymond, he had discounted everything in advance—everything except this worst of all foreseeable possibilities, her complete indifference.

"In those days I lived in a world of my own, and read the infinite into all sorts of nonsensical trifles. It is as though you were talking to me of some perfectly strange woman."

He knew that anger and hatred are but extensions of love, that if he could have roused them in Maria Cross his cause would not have been entirely hopeless. But the only effect his words had had upon this woman was to irritate her, to make her feel ashamed at the thought that once she had been caught out with such a wretched trick and in such paltry company.

"So you actually thought," she went on, "that a piece of silliness like that could mean something to me?"

He muttered that it had certainly meant something to him—an admission that he had never before made to himself, but now, at last, scarcely knowing what he said, put into words. He had no idea that the whole pattern of his life had been changed by that one squalid incident of his youth. He was caught in an uprush of suffering. He heard Maria's calm, detached voice:

"How right Bertrand is to say that we don't really begin to live until we've reached twenty-five or thirty."

He had a confused feeling that the remark was not true; that by the time we are beginning to grow up the future is wholly formed in us. On the threshold of manhood the bets have already been placed; nothing more can be staked. Inclinations planted in our flesh even before birth are inextricably confused with the innocence of our early years, but only when we have reached man's estate do they suddenly put forth their monstrous flowers.

Completely at sea, fighting his losing battle against this inaccessible woman, he remembered now what it was that he had so longed to tell Maria, and even though he realized increasingly as he spoke that his words were about as ill-timed as they possibly could be, declared that "our little adventure certainly hasn't stood in the way of my learning about love." Oh, very far from it! He was quite sure that he had had more women than any young man of his age—and women who had something to them, not just your common-or-garden tarts. . . . In that respect she had brought him luck.

She leaned back and, through half-closed eyes, looked at him with an expression of disgust. What, then, she asked, was he complaining of?

"Since, I presume, that sort of filth is the only thing you care about."

She lit a cigarette, leaned her cropped neck against the wall, and watched, through the smoke, the gyrations of three couples. When the jazz players paused for breath the men detached themselves from their partners, clapped their hands, and then stretched them toward the Negro instrumentalists in a gesture of supplication—as though their very lives depended upon a renewal of the din. The Negroes, moved by compassion, resumed their playing, and the May flies, borne aloft on the rhythm, clasped one another in a fresh embrace and once again took wing. But Raymond, with hatred in his heart, looked at this woman with the short hair and the cigarette, who was none other than Maria Cross. He searched for the one word that would shake her self-control, and at last he found it.

"Well, anyhow, you're—here."

She realized that what he meant was—we always return to our first loves. He had the satisfaction of seeing her cheeks flush to a deep red, her brows draw together in a harsh frown.

"I have always loathed places like this. To say that sort of thing shows how little you know me! Your father, I am sure, remembers the agonies I went through when Monsieur Larousselle used to drag me off to the Lion Rouge. It wouldn't be of the slightest use my telling you that the only thing that brings me here is a sense of duty—yes, of duty. . . . But what can a man like you know of my scruples? It was Bertrand himself who advised me to yield—within reason—to my husband's tastes. If I am to retain any influence, I mustn't ride him on too tight a rein. Bertrand is very broad-minded. He begged me not to resist his father's wish that I should cut my hair. . . ."

She had mentioned Bertrand's name merely in order to lessen her nervous tension, to feel at peace and mollified. By the light of memory, Raymond saw once again a deserted path in the Public Park in Bordeaux. The time was four o'clock. He could hear the panting of a small boy running after him, the sound of a tear-thickened voice: "Give me back my notebook." What sort of a man had that delicate youth become? Intent on wounding, he said:

"So you've got a grown-up son now?"

But she wasn't wounded at all; she smiled happily:

"Of course, you knew him at school. . . ."

Raymond suddenly took on for her a real existence. He had been one of Bertrand's schoolfellows.

"Yes, a grown-up son, but a son who can be at once a friend and a master. You cannot imagine how much I owe to him. . . ."

"You told me—your marriage."

"Oh *that!* . . . my marriage is the least of my debts. You see, he has revealed—but it's no good, you wouldn't understand. It was only that I was thinking how you'd known him at school. I'd so much like to have some idea of what he was like as a little boy. I've often asked my husband about him, but it's extraordinary how little a man can tell one about his son's childhood: 'A nice little chap, just like all the others'—that's as much as he can say. I've no reason to believe that you were any more observant. In the first place, you were much older than he was."

"Four years—that's nothing," Raymond muttered, and added: "I remember that he had a face like a girl."

She showed no sign of anger, but answered with quiet contempt that of course they could not have had much in common. Raymond realized that in the eyes of Maria Cross her stepson floated in an airy world far above his head. She was thinking of Bertrand: she had been drinking champagne; there was a rapturous smile upon her lips. Like the disunited May flies, she, too, clapped her hands, eager for the music to renew its spell about her. What remained in Raymond's memory of the women he had possessed? Some of them he would scarcely have recognized. But hardly a day had passed during the last seventeen years that he had not conjured up in his mind, had not insulted and caressed, the face which tonight he could see in profile close beside him. He could not endure that she should be so far from him in spirit. At all costs he must bridge the gap, and to that end he took the conversation back to Bertrand.

"I suppose he'll be leaving college very soon now?"

She replied with a show of polite interest that he was in his last year. He had lost four years because of the war. She hoped that he would graduate very high, and when Raymond remarked that no doubt Bertrand would follow in his father's footsteps, said, with some animation, that he must be given time in which to make up his mind. She was quite sure, she added, that he would make his influence felt no matter what profession he adopted. Raymond could not make out in what way he was so remarkable.

"The effect he has on his fellow students is quite extraordinary. . . . But I don't know why I am telling you all this. . . ."

She gave the impression that she was coming down to earth, coming down a long way, when she asked:

"And what about you. What do *you* do?"

"Oh, I just potter about, in the business world, you know."

It was suddenly borne in on him what a wretched mess he had made of his life. But she was barely listening. It wasn't that she despised him—that, in its way, would have been something definite, but that for her he simply did not exist. She half rose from her chair and made signs to Larousselle who was still holding forth from his stool. "Just a few more minutes!" he called back. In a low voice she said, "How red he looks—he's drinking too much."

The musicians were packing up their instruments with as much care as though they had been sleeping children. Only the piano seemed incapable of stopping. A single couple was revolving on the floor. The other dancers, their arms still intertwined, had collapsed onto seats. This was the moment of the evening which Raymond Courrèges had so often sipped and savored, the moment when claws are retracted, when eyes become veiled by a sudden softness, when voices sink to a whisper and hands become insidiously inviting. . . . There had been a time when, at such moments, he had smiled to himself, thinking of what was to come later, of men walking homeward in the early dawn, whistling to themselves and leaving behind, in the secrecy of some anonymous bedroom, a jaded body sprawled across a bed, so still, so spent, that it might have been that of a murdered woman. . . . Not thus would he have left the body of Maria Cross! A whole lifetime would have been all too short to satisfy his ravenous hunger.

So completely indifferent was she to his presence that she did not even notice how he had moved his leg closer to her own, did not even feel the contact. He had no power whatever over her. And yet in those distant years he had been hers for the taking. She had thought she loved him—and he had never known. He had been an inexperienced boy. She should have explained what it was she wanted of him. No whim, however extravagant, would have rebuffed him. He would have proceeded as slowly as she wished. He could, at need, make smooth and easy the voyage of pleasure . . . it would have brought her joy. But now it was too late. Centuries might pass before their ways should cross again in the six o'clock trolley. . . . He looked up and saw in a mirror the wreckage of his youth, the first sure signs of creeping age. Gone were the days when women might have loved him. Now it was for him to take the initiative, if, indeed, he were still worthy of love.

He laid his hand on hers:

"Do you remember the trolley?"

She shrugged her shoulders, and, without so much as turning her head, had the effrontery to ask:

"What trolley?"

Then, before he could reply, she hurried on:

"I wonder whether you would be so very kind as to bring Monsieur Larousselle over here and get his coat for him from the cloakroom . . . otherwise we shall never make a move."

He seemed not to have heard her. She had asked that question, "What trolley?" quite deliberately. He would have liked to protest that nothing in his whole life had ever meant so much to him as those moments when they had sat facing one another in a crowd of poor workpeople with coal-blackened faces and heads drooping with sleep. He could see the scene in imagination—a newspaper slipping to the floor from a hand gone numb; a bareheaded woman holding up her novelette to catch the light of the lamps, her lips moving as though in prayer. He could hear again the great raindrops splashing in the dust of the lane behind the church at Talence, could watch the passing figure of a workman crouched over the handlebar of his bicycle, a canvas sack, with a bottle protruding from it, slung over his shoulder. The trees behind the railings were stretching out their dusty leaves like hands begging for water.

"Do, please, go and fetch my husband. He's not used to drinking so much. I ought to have stopped him. Liquor is so bad for him."

Raymond, who had resumed his seat, got up again and, for the second time, shuddered at what he saw reflected in the mirror. He was still young, but what good would that do him? True, he might still awaken love, but no longer could he choose in whom. To a man who can still flaunt the passing glories of the body's springtime, everything is possible. Had his age been five years less than it was, he might, he thought, have had a chance. Better than most he knew what mere youthfulness can achieve with a woman who has been drained dry, how magically it can overcome antipathies and preferences, shame and remorse, what pricking curiosity, what appetites it can wake. But now he was without a weapon. Looking at himself he felt as a man might who goes into battle with a broken sword.

"If you won't do what I ask, I suppose I must go myself. They're making him drink. . . . I don't know how I can manage to get him away. How disgusting it all is!"

"What would your Bertrand say if he could see you now, sitting here with me . . . and his father in that state?"

"He would understand everything: he *does* understand everything."

It was at that moment that the noise of a heavy body crashing to the ground came from the bar. Raymond rushed across the room and, with the help of the barman, tried to lift Victor Larousselle, whose feet were caught in the overturned stool. His hand, streaming with blood, still convulsively clutched a broken bottle. Maria tremblingly threw a coat round the shoulders of Bertrand's father, and turned up the collar so as to hide his now purple face. The barman said to Raymond, who was settling the bill, that one could never be sure it wasn't a heart attack, and half carried the great hulking body to a taxi, so terrified was he of seeing a customer die before he had got clear of the premises.

Maria and Raymond, perched on the bracket seats, held the drunken creature in a sitting position. A bloodstain was slowly spreading over the handkerchief which they had wrapped round the injured hand. "This has never happened to him before," Maria moaned. "I ought to have remembered that he can't touch anything but wine. Swear you won't breathe a word of this to anyone." Raymond's mood was exultant. In an access of joy he greeted this unexpected turn in his affairs. No, nothing could have parted him from Maria Cross this evening. What a fool he had been to doubt his lucky star!

Although winter was on the wane, the night was cold. A powdering of sleet showed white on the Place de la

Concorde under the moon. He continued to hold up on the back seat the vast mass of flesh from which came the sound of hiccups and a confused burble of speech. Maria had opened a bottle of smelling salts. The young man adored their faint scent of vinegar. He warmed himself at the flame of the beloved body at his side, and took advantage of the brief flicker of each passing street lamp to take his fill of the face that looked so lovely in its humiliation. At one moment, when she took the old man's heavy and revolting head between her hands, she looked like Judith.

More than anything she dreaded that the porter might be a witness of the scene, and was only too glad of Raymond's offer to help her drag the sick man to the elevator. Scarcely had they got him on to his bed than they saw that his hand was bleeding freely, and that only the whites of his eyes were visible. Maria was worse than useless. She seemed quite incapable of doing the simplest things that would have come naturally to other women. . . . Must she wake the servants, who slept on the seventh floor? . . . What a scandal there would be! She decided to ring up her doctor. But he must have taken off the receiver, for she could get no answer. She burst into sobs. It was then that Raymond, remembering his father's presence in Paris, had the happy idea of ringing him, and suggested to Maria that he should do so. Without so much as a "Thank you," she started to hunt through the directory for the number of the Grand Hotel.

"He'll come as soon as he gets dressed and finds a taxi."

This time Maria did take his hand. She opened a door and switched on the light.

"Would you mind waiting in here: it's Bertrand's room." She said that the patient had been sick and felt better. But his hand was still giving him a good deal of pain.

As soon as she had left the room Raymond sat down and buttoned his overcoat. The radiator was not giving much heat. His father's sleepy voice was still in his ears. How far away it had sounded. They had not seen one another since old Grandmamma Courrèges had died three years before. At that time Raymond had been in pressing need of money. Perhaps there had been something rude and aggressive in the way he had demanded his share of the inheritance, but what had really got under his skin and precipitated a rupture had been the way in which his father lectured him on the subject of his choice of a profession. The mixture of cadging and pimping by which he had elected to earn a living had horrified the elder man, who regarded such an occupation as being unworthy of a Courrèges. He had gone so far as to try to extract a promise from Raymond that he would find some regular occupation. And now, in a few moments, he would be here, in this apartment. What ought his son to do—kiss him, or merely offer him his hand?

He tried to find an answer to the question, but all the time his attention was being drawn to, was being held by, one particular object in the room—Bertrand Larousselle's bed, a narrow iron bed, so unaccommodating, so demure beneath its flowered cotton coverlet that Raymond could not keep himself from bursting out laughing. It was the bed of an elderly spinster or a seminarist. Three of the walls were quite bare, the fourth was lined with books. The worktable was as neat as a good conscience. If Maria came to my place, she'd get a bit of a shock, he thought. She would see a divan so low that it seemed part of the floor. Every woman who ventured into that discreetly dimmed interior was at once conscious of a dangerous sense of being in some strange new world, of a temptation to indulge in activities which would no more commit her than if they had taken place in a different planet—or in the innocent privacy of sleep. . . . But in the room where Raymond was now waiting, no curtains hid the windows frosted by the winter night. Its owner wished, no doubt, that the light of dawn should wake him before the sounding of the earliest bell. Raymond was entirely insensitive to all the evidences of a life of purity. In this room designed for prayer he could see merely a cunning piece of trickery, a deliberate exploitation of refusal, of denial, designed to increase the delights of love by suppressing all obvious allurements. He looked at the titles of some of the books. "What an ass!" he murmured. These volumes that spoke of another world were quite outside his experience and gave him a feeling of disgust. . . . What a time his father was taking! He did not want to be alone much longer. The room seemed to mock at him. He opened the windows and looked out at the roofs beneath a late moon.

"Here's your father."

He closed the window, followed Maria into Victor Larousselle's room, saw a figure bending over the bed, and recognized his father's huge bowler hat lying on a chair, and the ivory-knobbed stick (which had been his horse in the days when he had played at horses). When the doctor raised his head he hardly knew him. Yet he realized that this old man who smiled and put his arm about his shoulder was his father.

"No tobacco, no spirits, no coffee. Poultry at lunch and no butcher's meat at night. Do as I say, and you'll live to be a hundred. . . . That's all."

The doctor repeated the words "That's all," in the drawling voice of a man whose thoughts are elsewhere. His eyes never left Maria's face. She, seeing him standing there motionless, took the initiative, opened the door, and said:

"I think what we all need is a good night's sleep."

The doctor followed her into the hall. Very shyly he said: "It was a bit of luck, our meeting like this." All the time he had been hurriedly dressing, and later, in the taxi, he had been quite convinced that as soon as he had said that Maria would break in with—"Now I've found you again, doctor, I'm not going to let you get away so easily." But that wasn't at all the answer she had made when, from the open door, he had eagerly remarked, "It was a bit of luck. . . ." Four times he repeated the phrase he had so carefully prepared, as though by stressing it he could force from her the hoped-for answer. But no; she just held up his overcoat and did not even show signs of impatience when he failed to find the sleeve. Quite unemotionally she said:

"It really is a very small world. This evening has brought us together after many years. It is more than likely that we shall meet again."

She pretended not to hear him when he said: "But don't you think it is up to us to put a spoke in fortune's wheel?"

He repeated the same remark more loudly: "Don't you think we might manage to put a spoke in fortune's wheel?"

If the dead could come back how embarrassing they would be! They do come back sometimes, treasuring an image of us which we long to destroy, their minds full of memories which we passionately desire to forget. These drowned bodies that are swept in by the flooding tide are a constant source of awkwardness to the living.

"I am very different from the lazy creature whom you once knew, doctor. I want to get to bed, because I've got to be up by seven."

She felt irritated by him for saying nothing. She had a sense of discomfort beneath the brooding stare of this old man who merely went on repeating: "Don't you think we might put a spoke in fortune's wheel?"

She replied with a good grace, though rather brusquely, that he had her address.

"I scarcely ever go to Bordeaux these days; but perhaps you . . ."

It had been so kind of him to take all this trouble.

"If the staircase light goes out, you'll find the switch *there*."

He made no movement, but stayed obstinately where he was. Did she never, he asked, feel any ill effects from her fall?

Raymond emerged from the shadows: "What fall was that?"

She made a gesture with her head expressive of utter exhaustion.

"What would really give me pleasure, doctor, would be to think that we could write to one another. I'm not the letter writer I used to be . . . but for you . . ."

He replied: "Letters are worse than useless. What's the point of writing if we are never to see one another?"

"But that's precisely the reason."

"No, no. Do you think that if people knew they were never going to see one another again they would want to prolong their friendship artificially by corresponding, especially if one of the two realized that letter writing imposed a dreary duty on the other? . . . One becomes a coward, Maria, as one grows older. One has had one's life and one dreads fresh disappointments."

He had never put his feelings so clearly into words. Surely she would understand now!

Her attention had strayed because Larousselle was calling for her, because it was five o'clock, because she wanted to get rid of the Courrèges'.

"Well, *I* shall write to *you,* doctor, and you shall have the dreary duty of replying."

But a little later, when she had locked and bolted the door and gone back to the bedroom, her husband heard her laugh and asked what she was laughing at.

"The most extraordinary thing's just occurred to me . . . promise you won't mock. I really believe that the doctor was a bit in love with me in the old Bordeaux days . . . it wouldn't surprise me."

Victor Larousselle replied thickly through clammy lips that he wasn't jealous if that was what she meant, and followed up the remark with one of his hoariest jokes: "He's just ripe for the cold stone." He added that the poor fellow had obviously had a slight stroke. Many of his old patients, who didn't like to abandon him, secretly consulted other doctors.

"Not feeling sick any longer? Sure your hand doesn't hurt?"

No, he was quite comfortable.

"I only hope that the story of what happened tonight doesn't make the rounds in Bordeaux. . . . Young Courrèges is quite capable . . ."

"He never goes there nowadays. Try to get some sleep. I'm going to put out the light."

She sat in the darkness, motionless, until a sound of quiet snoring rose from the bed. Then she went to her room, passing, on the way, Bertrand's half-open door. She could not resist the temptation to push it wide. Standing on the threshold she sniffed. The mingled smell of tobacco and the human body filled her with a cold fury: I must have been mad to let him come in here! . . . She opened the windows to let in the cold air of dawn, and knelt down for a moment at the head of the bed. Her lips moved. She buried her face in the pillow.

12

THE DOCTOR and Raymond drove away in a taxi. It was like the old days when they had sat together in the carriage with its streaming windows on a suburban road. At first they said no more to one another than they had used to do in that forgotten time. But there was a difference in the quality of their silence. The old man was sagging with weariness and leaned against his son. Raymond held his hand.

"I had no idea that she was married."

"They didn't tell anybody: at least, I believe and hope that they didn't. They certainly didn't tell me."

It was said that young Bertrand had insisted on the situation being regularized. The doctor quoted a remark made by Victor Larousselle: "I am making a morganatic marriage." Raymond muttered: "What dam' cheek!" He stole a glance in the half-light at the tormented face beside him, and saw that the bloodless lips were moving. The frozen expression, the features looking as though they were carved in stone, frightened him. He said the first thing that came into his head.

"How's everybody?"

Flourishing. Madeleine, in particular, said the doctor, was

being splendid. She lived for nothing but her two girls, took them out to parties, and hid her sorrow from the world, showing herself worthy of the hero she had lost. (The doctor never neglected an opportunity of praising the son-in-law who had been killed at Guise, striving, in this way, to make honorable amends for the past. He blamed himself for having been wrong about him. So many men in the war had been surprisingly unlike themselves in death.) Catherine, Madeleine's eldest daughter, was engaged to the Michon boy, the youngest of three brothers, but there was to be no public announcement until she was twenty-two:

"You mustn't breathe a word about it."

The voice in which he uttered this injunction was his wife's, and Raymond caught back the words he had been about to say: "Why should anyone in Paris be interested?" The doctor broke off as though suddenly silenced by a stab of pain. The young man began silently to calculate: He must be sixty-nine or seventy. Is it possible to go on suffering at that age, and after all these years? . . . He became suddenly aware of his own hurt, and the consciousness of it frightened him. It wouldn't last . . . very soon it would pass into forgetfulness. He remembered something that one of his mistresses had said: "When I'm in love and going through hell, I just curl up and wait. I know that in a very short while the particular man in question will mean absolutely nothing to me, though at the moment I may be ready to die for him, that I shan't so much as spare a passing glance for the cause of so much suffering. It's terrible to love, and humiliating to stop loving. . . ." All the same, this old man had been bleeding from a mortal wound for seventeen long years. In lives like his, hedged about with routine, dominated by a sense of duty, passion becomes concentrated, is put away, as it were, in cold storage. There is no way of using it up, no breath of warm air can reach it and start the process of evaporation. It grows and grows, stagnates, corrupts, poisons, and corrodes the living flesh that holds it prisoner.

They swung round the Arc de Triomphe. Between the puny trees of the Champs Élysées the black road flowed on like Erebus.

"I think I've done with pottering around. I've been offered a job in a factory. They make chicory. At the end of a year I shall be managing director."

The doctor's reply was perfunctory: "I'm so glad, my boy." Suddenly he shot a question: "How did you first meet?"

"Meet whom?"

"You know perfectly well what I mean."

"The friend who offered me this job?"

"Of course not—Maria."

"It goes back a long way. When I was in my last term at school, we got to exchanging a few words in the trolley. I think that's how it all began."

"You never told me, though once, if I remember correctly, you did mention that some friend had pointed her out to you in the street."

"Perhaps I did . . . one's memory gets a bit hazy after seventeen years. Yes, it all comes back now: it was the day after that meeting that she first spoke to me—actually, it was to ask after you. She knew me by sight. I think that if her husband hadn't come over to me this evening she'd have cut me."

This brief interchange seemed to have set the doctor's mind at rest. He leaned back in his corner. He muttered: "Anyhow, what does it matter to me? What does it matter?" He made the old familiar gesture of sweeping away some obstacle, rubbed his cheeks, sat up and half turned toward Raymond in an effort to escape from his thoughts, to occupy his mind only with his son's concerns.

"As soon as you've got an assured position, my boy, hurry up and get married."

Raymond laughed, protested, and the old man was once more driven in upon himself:

"You can have no idea what a comfort it is to live in the middle of a large family. Yes, I mean it. One's all the time got to think about other people's troubles, and those thousands of little hypodermic pricks keep the blood flowing. Do you see what I mean? One has no time to think of one's own secret miseries, of the wounds that strike deep into the very roots of one's being. One gets to rely on all these family concerns. . . . For instance, I meant to stay in Paris until the end of the Conference, but I've suddenly decided to catch the eight o'clock train this morning. I just can't help myself. The great thing in life is to make some sort of refuge for oneself. At the end of one's existence, as at the beginning, one's got to be borne by a woman."

Raymond mumbled something about rather seeing himself dead first. He looked at the shrunken, moth-eaten old figure at his side.

"You can have no idea how safe I've always felt with all of you round me. To have a wife, children, about one, pressing in on one, is a sort of protection against all the undesirable distractions of outside life. You never used to say much to me—I don't mean that as a reproach, dear boy—but I don't think you'll ever realize how often, just as I was on the point of yielding to some delicious, maybe criminal, temptation, I would feel your hand on my shoulder gently guiding me back into the right path."

"How ridiculous to think that there are such things as forbidden pleasures," Raymond muttered. "We're completely different, you and I; I'd have overturned the whole applecart in next to no time."

"You're not the only one who made your mother suffer. We're not really so different. Scores of times I've sent the applecart spinning—in imagination. You don't know. . . . No, you *don't.* A few casual infidelities would have brought me far less sorrow than the long-drawn-out disloyalty of desire of which I have been guilty for the last thirty years. It is essential that you should know all this, Raymond. You'd find it pretty difficult to be a worse husband than I have been. Oh, I know my orgies never went beyond daydreaming, but does that make it any better? The way your mother takes her revenge now is by being overattentive. Her fussing has become a necessity of my existence. The endless trouble to which she goes. She never lets me out of her sight day or night. I shall die in the lap of comfort, never fear. We're not looked after now as we used to be. Servants, as she says, are no longer what they were. We've never replaced Julie—do you remember Julie? She's gone back to her native village. Your mother does everything. I have to scold her, often. There's nothing she won't turn her hand to—sweeping out the rooms, polishing the floors."

He stopped, then, with a note of supplication in his voice: "Don't live alone," he said.

Raymond had no time to reply. The taxi stopped in front of the Grand Hotel. He had to get out, feel for his money. The doctor had only just enough time to do his packing.

These early hours of the morning, all given over to street sweepers and market gardeners, were familiar to Raymond Courrèges. He breathed in the dawn air, rejoicing in the well-known sights, remembering how he always felt as he walked home in the small hours, physically exhausted, his senses gorged and satisfied, happy as a young animal wanting nothing but to find its burrow, to curl up and sleep. What a blessing that his father had decided to say good-bye at the door of the Grand Hotel. How he had aged! How he had shrunk! There can never be too many miles for my liking, between me and the family, he thought: The farther away one's relations, the better. . . . It came over him that he was no longer thinking about Maria. He remembered that he had a whole lot of things to do today. He took out his engagement book, turned the pages, and was amazed to discover how vast the day had become—or was it that the things with which he had proposed to fill it had diminished in number? The morning?—an empty waste: the afternoon? —two appointments which he had no intention of keeping.

He leaned over his day like a child over the rim of a well. Only a few pebbles to drop into it, and *they* wouldn't fill the yawning void. Only one thing could do that—going to see Maria, being announced, being welcomed, sitting in the same room with her, talking to her—it wouldn't matter about what. Even less than that would have sufficed to fill these empty hours and many, many more—even just to have known that he had arranged a meeting with her, no matter how far ahead it might be. With the patience of a marksman, he would have shot down the days separating him from that longed-for moment. Even if she had put him off, he would have found comfort somehow—provided she had suggested an alternative date, and the new hope thus started on its way would have been enough to fill the infinite emptiness of his life. For life now had become for him nothing but a feeling of absence which he had got to balance by a feeling of anticipation. "I must think the whole business out seriously," he told himself, "and begin only with what is possible. Why shouldn't I get in touch with Bertrand again and worm my way into his life?" But they had no single taste in common, did not even know the same people. Anyhow, where was he to find him?—in what sacristy run this sacristan to earth? In imagination he obliterated all the intervening stages which separated him from Maria, jumped the gap, and reached the point at which he was holding that mysterious head in the crook of his right arm. He could feel on his biceps the touch of her shaven neck, like the cheek of a young boy. Her face swam toward him, closer, closer, enormously enlarged as on a movie screen, and no less intangible. . . . It struck him with amazement that the early wayfarers he met did not turn to look at him, did not notice his mania. How well our clothes conceal our real selves! He dropped on to a seat opposite the Madeleine. This seeing her again . . . that was the trouble. He ought never to have seen her again. All the passions in which he had indulged for seventeen years had, unknown to him, been lit to protect himself from her—as the peasants of the Landes start small fires to keep the greater fire from spreading. . . . But he *had* seen her, and the fire had got the better of him, had been increased by the flames with which he had thought to combat it. His sensual aberrations, his secret vices, the cold technique of self-indulgence, so patiently learned, so carefully cultivated, all had added fuel to the conflagration, so that it roared upward now, sweeping toward him on a vast front with a sound of crackling undergrowth.

"Lie low, curl yourself up into a ball," he kept on saying to himself. "It won't last, and until it's over, find some drug with which to stupefy yourself—float with the current." Yes, but—his father would know no lessening of *his* pain until the day of his death. What a dreary life he'd led! But would a course of debauchery have freed him from his passion?—that was the question. Everything serves as fuel for passion: abstinence sharpens it; repletion strengthens it; virtue keeps it awake and irritates it. It terrifies and it fascinates. But if we yield, our cowardice is never abject enough to satisfy its exigence. It is a frantic and a horrible obsession. He should have asked his father how on earth he had managed to live with that cancer gnawing at his vitals. . . . Of what use is a virtuous existence? What way of escape can it provide? What power has God over passion?

He concentrated his attention on the minute hand of the great clock away to his left, trying to catch it in the act of moving. By this time, he thought, his father must already have left the hotel. He suddenly felt that he would like to give the old man one last kiss. There was more than paternity between them, there was another tie of blood. They were related in their common feeling for Maria Cross. . . .

Raymond hastened toward the river, though there was plenty of time before the train was due to leave. Perhaps he was yielding to that species of madness which compels those whose clothes have caught fire to run. He was oppressed by the intolerable conviction that he would never possess Maria Cross, that he would die without ever having her. Though he had had his will of many women, taken them, held them for a while, abandoned them, he felt himself to be in the grip of the same sort of wild despair which sometimes overwhelms men who have never known physical love, men condemned to a life of virginity, when they face the horror of dying without ever having known the delights of the flesh. What he had had in the past no longer counted. Nothing seemed worth the having save what he would never have.

Maria! He was appalled to think how heavily one human being may, without wishing it, weigh in the scales of another's destiny. He had never given a thought to those virtues which, radiating from ourselves, operate, often without our knowing it and often over great distances, on the hearts of others. All the way along the pavement that stretches between the Tuileries and the Seine he found himself, for the first time in his life, compelled to think about things to which, up till then, he had never given a moment's consideration. Probably because on the threshold of this new day he felt emptied of all ambitions, of all plans, of all possible amusements, he found that there was nothing now to keep his mind from the life that lay behind him. Because there was no longer any future to which he might look forward, the past swarmed into his mind. For how many living creatures had not his mere proximity meant death and destruction? Even now he did not know to what lives he had given purpose and direction, what lives he had cut adrift from their moorings; did not know that because of him some woman had killed the young life just stirring in her womb; that because of him a young girl had died, a friend had gone into a seminary; and that each of these single dramas had given birth to others in an endless succession. On the brink of this appalling emptiness, of this day without Maria, which was to be but the first of many other days without her, he was made aware, at one and the same moment, of his dependence and his solitude. He felt himself forced into the closest possible communion with a woman with whom he would never make contact. It was enough that her eyes should see the light for Raymond to live forever in the darkness. For how long? If he decided that, at no matter what cost, he must fight his way out of the dense blackness, must escape from this murderous law of gravity, what choices were there open to him but the alternatives of stupor or of sleep?

—unless this star in the firmament of his heart should go suddenly dead, as all love goes dead. He carried within him a tearing, frantic capability of passion, inherited from his father—of a passion that was all-powerful, that would breed, until he died, still other planetary worlds, other Maria Crosses, of which, in succession, he would become the miserable satellite. . . . There could be no hope for either of them, for father or for son, unless, before they died, He should reveal Himself who, unknown to them, had drawn and summoned from the depths of their beings this burning, bitter tide.

He crossed the deserted Seine and looked at the station clock. By this time his father must be in the train. He went down on to the departure platform and walked along the row of waiting coaches. He did not have to search for long. Through the glass of one of the windows he saw the corpse-like face etched on the darkness of the interior. The eyes were closed, the clasped hands lay on a spread of newspaper, the head leaned slightly backward, the mouth was half open. Raymond tapped with his finger. The corpse opened its eyes, recognized the source of the sound, smiled, and, with uncertain steps, came out into the corridor. But all the doctor's happiness was ruined by his childish fear that the train might start before Raymond had had time to get out.

"Now that I've seen you, now that I know you wanted to see *me* again, my mind is at rest. Better go now, dear boy. They're closing the doors."

It was in vain that the young man assured him that they had a good five minutes before the train would start, and that, in any case, it stopped at the Austerlitz station. The other continued to show signs of nervousness until his son was once more safely on the platform. Then, lowering the window, he gazed long and lovingly at him.

Raymond asked him whether he had got everything he wanted. Would he like another paper or a book? Had he reserved a seat in the restaurant car? To all these questions the doctor replied, "Yes, yes." Hungrily he fixed his eyes on the young man who had asked them; the man who was so different from himself, and yet so like him—the part of his own flesh and blood that would survive him for a few more years, but that he was fated never to see again.

CARROLL & GRAF